"Being alone isn't a

Ryan turned toward the front window. His shoulders tensed when he peered out. He whirled around. "Get down!" He wrapped an arm around Catherine's back and took her to the floor.

Betty rose from where she was resting and barked. Liz paced.

The front window shattered, spraying glass across the wood floor.

Catherine shook her head, not comprehending.

"He found us," said Ryan.

His words reverberated in her brain. The guy had some tracking skills. She wasn't safe here or on the mountain. Though the cabin was partially hidden by trees, the ATV with its distinct dog carrier was parked outside. Denial still swirled through her thoughts. This could not be happening. The safe world she'd created was being ripped away from her.

"My car is parked on the side of the cabin," she said. "There's a back door." She called the dogs to her.

"Stay low." Ryan pulled his gun from its holster as a second shot rang out...

Ever since she found the Nancy Drew books with the pink covers in her country school library, **Sharon Dunn** has loved mystery and suspense. Most of her books take place in Montana, where she lives with three nearly grown children and a hyper border collie. She lost her beloved husband of twenty-seven years to cancer in 2014. When she isn't writing, she loves to hike surrounded by God's beauty.

Books by Sharon Dunn

Love Inspired Suspense

Big Sky Showdown
Hidden Away
In Too Deep
Wilderness Secrets
Mountain Captive
Undercover Threat
Alaskan Christmas Target
Undercover Mountain Pursuit
Crime Scene Cover-Up
Christmas Hostage
Montana Cold Case Conspiracy
Montana Witness Chase
Kidnapped in Montana

Alaska K-9 Unit

Undercover Mission

Pacific Northwest K-9 Unit

Threat Detection

Visit the Author Profile page at LoveInspired.com for more titles.

Kidnapped in Montana

SHARON DUNN

LOVE INSPIRED SUSPENSE
INSPIRATIONAL ROMANCE

LOVE INSPIRED® SUSPENSE

INSPIRATIONAL ROMANCE

ISBN-13: 978-1-335-59813-4

Kidnapped in Montana

Recycling programs
for this product may
not exist in your area.

Love Inspired
22 Adelaide St. West, 41st Floor
Toronto, Ontario M5H 4E3, Canada
www.LoveInspired.com

Printed in Lithuania

MIX
Paper | Supporting
responsible forestry
FSC® C021394

Trust in the Lord with all thine heart; and lean not unto thine own understanding. In all thy ways acknowledge him, and he shall direct thy paths.
—*Proverbs* 3:5–6

This book is dedicated to the border collie in my life, Bart, because there is never a dull moment when you are around.

ONE

FBI Agent Ryan McCloud wiped the drizzle from the visor of his helmet and stared at the winding mountain trail below. Though the rain smeared the view of what lay at the bottom of the road, he could just make out a faint, round dot of light. Probably a lantern inside a tent. Signs of an encampment. His destination.

His job as an agent took him all over the world into all kinds of situations, but riding an ATV in the Montana wilderness to track down an informant was a first. Victoria Stevenson had been feeding him information about an international gem smuggling ring operating out of the Seattle area. Two months ago, she'd disappeared. *Missing... presumed dead* was what the police report said.

Two things gave Ryan pause in believing the official report. His gut and the fact that half a million in diamonds was rumored to have disappeared at the same time. Had Victoria feared for her life and gone into hiding, taking the diamonds as collateral to set herself up somewhere safe? Had she switched sides? He didn't know. He simply could not let go of the feeling that she was still alive.

If she had betrayed him, it would be the second time in his work as an agent, not to mention the times women he was involved with romantically had been deceptive about who they were. He didn't trust himself anymore to be a good judge of character.

He twisted the throttle on the ATV. The back tire slipped a bit on the muddy trail. Though it was midday, the overcast sky made it seem darker. Springtime in Montana must mean lots of rain. His headlight cut a swath of illumination as the trail became more treacherous.

His search for Victoria had seemed futile until he caught a break. Facial identification software found a match for her. A woman in the background of a photo about the forest service working with conservation dogs and private landowners matched Victoria's facial features.

Victoria's change in profession came as a surprise. The article said that conservation dogs were trained to track the migratory habits of various predators and to sniff out rare plants. All done to make development of an area take into consideration the occupants who already called it home. Interesting work, but it didn't seem like anything Victoria would take to, though she had owned a border collie named Liz that disappeared at the same time she did. The article mentioned the use of the breed. It had to be her.

From her penthouse in Seattle, Victoria had been all high heels and business suits, so it was hard to picture her doing a job that led her far from people and food delivery. Maybe that was why she'd chosen it. No one would think to look for her here.

He slowed as the trail became even steeper. He heard a noise that sounded like another ATV coming around a bend behind him. Who else would be out in this weather? Maybe his ears were playing tricks on him.

Ryan made his way slowly down the mountain. As the encampment became more distinct, he could see a person in rain gear calling two border collies. Good sign. He could also see an ATV and a tent with a tarp over it. Boxes that looked waterproof were stacked around the tent.

A flash of light caught his attention in his peripheral vision. Another ATV was headed up the trail. To what purpose? The guy couldn't be out in this weather for pleasure. Maybe he was connected to the camp below, bringing supplies or something.

Ryan putted down the muddy mountain but stopped when the other ATV got close. He flipped up his visor. The guy was above him and far enough away that he had to shout.

"What brings you out here?"

The other rider idled but did not respond. He twisted the throttle and moved toward Ryan. His dark helmet hid his face. Unfriendliness in a setting with so few people seemed out of place. Then again, maybe some people chose the deep wilderness because they lacked social skills.

Wary of how muddy the trail had become, Ryan moved at a snail's pace as the other ATV drew closer. There was no need to create a traffic jam on such an isolated trail. Once again, he stopped, flipped up his visor, and shouted to be heard above the rain.

"Do you need to get past me? The trail is pretty narrow."

Still wearing his helmet, the other guy dismounted his ATV and stalked toward Ryan.

"Seriously, I'm not in a hurry, pal," said Ryan. "I'll get out of your way as soon as the trail is wide enough."

When he was within five yards of Ryan, the other man unzipped his leather jacket and reached inside.

The back of Ryan's neck prickled, a fear response.

A gun? What was going on here?

Ryan twisted the throttle and revved forward at a dangerous speed. He thought he heard a popping sound behind him. His heart pounded as he willed the vehicle to go faster and not wreck. He focused on the steep trail in front of him and tried to sort through why someone would be shooting at him.

Even if this was an angry landowner, it seemed like such an extreme response. The fat tires of the ATV slid and skidded as he increased his speed. His feet lifted from the pedals when he veered sideways, but he righted himself with a reactionary twist of the handlebars. The other rider had returned to his ATV and loomed toward him again.

Without warning, the tires froze up and Ryan found himself somersaulting through the air. His body banged against a hard surface and then he landed on his back. He was able to fight off unconsciousness for only a few seconds.

He could hear the hum and grind of the other ATV growing fainter as his world went black.

From her camp, Catherine Reed watched in horror as one of the two ATV riders sailed over the top of his vehicle. The ATV rolled and landed upright some distance from the trail. Though it was hard to see from where she stood, it looked like the rider had been thrown clear and now lay motionless in some brush. Only the bright yellow-and-blue stripes on his leather pants and jacket indicated where he was.

The headlights of the other ATV were not visible as it sunk down a hill and hadn't reached the rise yet.

Her muscles tensed as her heartbeat revved up a notch.

No one came up here. And certainly not under these conditions. Her first thought was the default explanation her mind always went to. Her abusive ex-husband David Reed had found her. And he'd brought a friend along to help keep his promise to kill her for leaving him.

The wreck victim still wasn't moving. Regardless of who he was, she couldn't leave him to die. She commanded her dogs to stay in the tent and mounted up on her own ATV heading toward the injured man.

Why had the other rider not come to the aid of the injured man? From the camp below, she had more of a panoramic view of the mountain above. Maybe the other man had not seen the accident.

The grass on the side of the hill provided some traction as she worked her way upward. Fear gripped her heart when she stopped several yards from where the man lay. What if this was her ex? She still had a moral obligation to render aid under such circumstances.

The scary thing was that her ex had found her despite her best efforts to go into hiding. She thought working with her conservation detection dog in remote places would keep her off the radar. There had been that news article where she'd been photographed in the background working with Betty, her border collie, while the forest ranger posed in the foreground. No one she worked with knew her story.

When the photographer suggested she and Betty pose with the forest ranger, she had made a quick excuse that it would be more interesting to see the dog in action. She thought she had turned quickly enough so that her face would barely show in profile. But someone looking for her might recognize her. Certainly, Betty's unique half white, half black coloring on her face would give her away to someone obsessed with finding her. Though she understood taking Betty with her when she'd fled created risk, she had not been able to leave the beloved dog behind. She feared what her ex might do to the dog out of revenge.

When Catherine was within yards of where the man lay on his back, she stopped, dismounted and hurried toward him. Her stomach knotted with fear. As she approached, the man still did not move. She kneeled beside him and shook his shoulder. No response.

She touched the side of his neck. He still had a pulse.

Catherine took in a breath and flipped up the visor bracing for a view of Dave's angry face. She sighed with relief when she saw that this man was a stranger to her.

She shook his shoulder again. Moving him would be dicey. If he had a back or neck injury, it would be made worse if she tried to transport him. Plus, she doubted she had the physical strength to lift him anyway. Being injured this far from medical help wasn't safe.

She said a quick prayer for the man but couldn't begin to assess his injuries until he was conscious.

She leaned over him. "Please wake up."

Yipping sounds, nearly drowned out by the wind and rain, drew her attention back down to the camp. She stood up to see better. The other ATV had arrived at her camp. Both dogs had come outside the tent. Betty ran circles around and barked at the man in the helmet as he overturned the boxes of supplies that were outside the tent, some under tarps. Liz, her other border collie, stood off to the side.

As the rain dripped off her face, Catherine couldn't comprehend what she was witnessing. The other rider was destroying her camp.

She watched in horror as the man pulled a gun from his leather jacket and aimed it toward the barking dogs. Betty retreated into the trees. Liz followed.

Catherine's breath caught.

When she turned back toward the injured man, he was sitting up.

She took two steps toward him placing her hands on her hips. "What is going on here?"

The man shook his head. Clearly not coherent yet.

"Why is that man tearing my camp to pieces and terrorizing my dogs? What are you two up to?"

The man tore his helmet off as rain pelted his sandy-colored hair. "Give me a second."

She fell to the ground and grabbed the collar of his leather jacket. "Did Dave Reed send you?"

The man shook his head. His forehead crinkled, and he looked at her with the bluest eyes she'd ever seen. "I don't know who you're talking about."

Did he think he could get away with such a lie? These men were clearly here to destroy her food supply and shelter and maybe hurt her. How dare they try to harm her dogs.

The man with the blue eyes grabbed her arm. "I came here for you. Whatever you've done, it's going to be okay."

His coat was half unzipped, revealing the handle of a gun in a holster. Fear enveloped her as she rose and took a step back shaking her head. "I doubt that."

She retreated toward the ATV with a backward glance at the man as he stumbled to his feet. She ran faster, reaching the four-wheeler and swinging her leg over.

The man was conscious. Her obligation to him as a fellow human being ended there. The gun suggested nefarious intent. She could not risk her own safety, and right now, her primary concern was the welfare of her dogs and getting away.

Catherine could hear the man shouting behind her as she rumbled down the hill. When she was far enough from the man who had wrecked his ATV, she killed the engine and lights on her ATV and hid in the brush. She had only a partial view of the activity below, but the other man who still wore his helmet had cut open her tent and upended everything inside.

The man was the same muscular build as Dave. Did he think destroying her camp and pouring out her supplies would lead to her demise?

Her thoughts turned to the dogs. They'd been smart enough to retreat into the trees. Hopefully, they weren't so frightened that they'd run far away. Betty was seasoned at surviving in the wilderness, but Liz was not.

Liz had been her twin sister Victoria's dog. Though she had not been close to her sister for years, they had an agreement that if something happened to one of them, the other would make sure the dog was taken care of.

When she'd been informed of Victoria's disappearance, she'd made arrangements for Liz to be shipped to her. Communication between the sisters had broken down years ago. Their parents' divorce when they were both thirteen meant Victoria had chosen to live in the city with her mother and Catherine had chosen to stay on the farm with her father, where they raised and trained border collies. The love of the dogs was probably the only thing the siblings still had in common.

Though she wasn't sure why her sister had disappeared, she didn't believe for a moment that Victoria was dead. Nothing broke the bond between two people who had been in the same womb for nine months. Catherine knew her sister was still alive…somewhere.

The man ransacking her camp stopped and turned, looking up the hill. Her breath hitched as she took a step back. She'd been spotted.

The helmeted man stalked toward his ATV and got on. He was heading right toward her.

When she looked over her shoulder, the other man, the one with the blue eyes, was coming toward her as well, though not very fast as he walked with a limp and hadn't made it to his ATV yet.

Catherine hurried toward her ATV and wasted no time hopping on and revving the engine. She had to escape—and fast.

TWO

Ryan knew he couldn't catch Victoria on foot. He must have twisted his ankle in the crash. Favoring his right foot, he burst into a sort of hopping run.

He wasn't sure what to make of Victoria's reaction to him. If she had stolen the diamonds, she probably knew he would have to take her in. He couldn't decipher the look on her face when she saw him. Guilt maybe. She must know that she had some leverage as an informant. Then again, he could interpret her expression as a more neutral response, like she was pretending not to know him. Victoria's acting skills were one of the things that had made her a great informant.

She had seemed genuine about wanting to stop the smuggling of precious gems from country to country, but maybe it was just too tempting to start playing for the other side. There was a turf war going on between mafia-backed smugglers and an unknown culprit that Victoria was trying to track down. The helmeted rider was probably working for one of the two forces at play.

Temptation and danger had been all around Victoria. She was a buyer for a high-end jewelry store. Her job took her all over the world and put her in contact with many people connected to the gem trade. She'd agreed to be an informant because to her way of thinking, the illegal trade in diamonds and other gems drove prices down for honest dealers. Ryan had acted as her handler but also had worked undercover as a store clerk and buyer trying to get to know the players in the jewelry-selling circles.

Ryan peered down at the scene below. If he wanted answers, he needed to catch Victoria and take her in.

Victoria traveled across the hillside as the other ATV gained on her. She appeared to be headed toward the trees that surrounded the open area where her destroyed campsite was.

The other ATV rider stopped and pulled a gun.

No. He wasn't about to watch her die.

Half running and half limping, he pulled his own gun and fired a shot in the direction of the ATV rider. The bullet pinged off something. The shot had been wild but was enough to draw the helmeted rider's attention away from Victoria for a second.

The guy aimed his gun at Ryan, who dropped to the ground.

The distraction had allowed Victoria to put some distance between herself and her pursuer. But his desire to protect her may have cost him the chance to take her in. He watched her disappear into the trees.

Though he had no idea who the Dave person she'd mentioned was, it was clear she was frightened of him.

The other rider returned to his ATV and headed in the direction Victoria had gone.

Ryan stumbled toward his own four-wheeler, which looked to be mired in the mud. As best as he could remember the crash, the ATV had rolled but ended up on the wheels. He swung is leg over the seat, said a quick prayer that it would start and turned the key in the ignition.

The motor made a grinding noise and then flared to life. He took in a breath and rolled down the hill back toward the trail. The other rider had just disappeared into the trees. Ryan followed, his ankle still hurting.

The overcast sky and canopy of trees made it seem like night instead of afternoon. The trail narrowed and then split off. He couldn't see either of the riders, though he could hear a mechanical hum that seemed to fade and then intensify. It was hard to tell where the sound was coming from as it echoed through the forest.

The cover of the trees kept the trail from getting too muddy, but there were no clear tracks to follow. He made a choice where the road forked, turned and kept going. His headlights cut a cone of light. After not seeing or hearing anything for at least five minutes, he stopped and turned the engine off.

A faint yipping noise reached his ears. A dog emerged from behind some brush. The animal had the same coloring as Victoria's dog, Liz. Three black legs and one white salt-and-pepper front leg. A white stripe divided Liz's face in half. Victoria had spoken very little about her family or her past. Only that her mother and father had bred border collies and that Liz was one of the last in the line.

Ryan flipped up his visor and called the dog's name. She came running to him tail wagging.

"Hey, remember me?"

He reached down and lifted the dog. The animal, wet and shivering, nuzzled close to him.

"You're kind of out of your element, aren't you? Used to a lot more pampering."

Grateful that Liz was on the small side, he unzipped his coat and put the sides of it around her to keep her warm.

He found a wide place to turn around and returned to

where the trail had split. He hadn't heard the other ATVs since he'd found the dog.

He rumbled down the trail as it became more twisty, not seeing or hearing anything that would indicate he was headed in the right direction.

He wondered if the helmeted rider was somehow connected to the people Victoria had taken the smuggled diamonds from…if she had taken them. The guy had clearly been searching for something in the camp.

The man had a gun. Would he simply kill Victoria for revenge or keep her alive long enough to find out where the jewels were? Maybe kidnap her so she could lead him to the stones.

In any case, he couldn't let that man get close to Victoria. He had to keep looking for her. Hopefully, he could find her before any harm came to her.

Catherine brought the ATV to a stop behind some brush and turned off the headlights. She had one advantage over the two men who were after her. She'd been up here long enough to easily navigate the labyrinth of trails, paths and open country that wove through this mountain.

She and Betty had been hired to track the migration patterns of the animals that lived in this area, the bear, the mountain lion and the wolf. If they could show that this was prime habitat for any of those animals, it would affect the choices the landowner made for development. The job meant she had been up here for months, retreating back to civilization only to get supplies. The forest service loaned her a cabin not too far from town where she could shower and regroup when needed.

Because of her knowledge of the landscape, she was confident she could dodge the two men on ATVs in the short term. What she was more worried about was finding the dogs. How deep into the forest had their fear driven them?

Betty would at some point return to the camp. She only hoped that Liz would tag along. Fearing the noise of the ATV would give her away, she opted instead to slip off the trail and work her way back to the camp on foot.

The two men had guns and that gave her pause. If she could find the dogs and get them loaded up before she was spotted, she'd be able to escape. There was more than one way off this mountain, and she was familiar with most of them.

She stepped through some brush and trees, her hiking boots padding lightly. Every rock and fallen log functioned like a signpost to her. It was easy enough to navigate through the forest to where she needed to be. She came to the edge of the trees and found a spot where she had a view of the camp. The sight of her destroyed camp tied her stomach in knots.

Behind her, she could hear an ATV, though it sounded far away. She kneeled down where the brush provided a nice hiding spot. After waiting about twenty minutes, Betty made an appearance, sniffing the overturned supplies and the torn tent. Catherine's spirits lifted at the sight of her dog.

Good girl.

Catherine glanced around. No sign of Liz.

One of the ATVs was getting louder and closer.

She whistled and Betty raised her head. "That's my girl," she whispered.

Betty rushed toward where Catherine was hidden. The dog leapt into Catherine's lap and licked her face. She drew the dog close. "You had a little scare, my friend. So glad you're safe."

She stroked the dog's muzzle and torso as the rumble of the ATV engine intensified. He was getting close.

"We gotta be quiet." She petted the dog's ear.

The vehicle lumbered by maybe ten feet from where she and Betty were hidden. Knowing the dog would give a warning bark out of habit, she wrapped her hand gently around Betty's muzzle.

She could feel the warmth of Betty's body against her chest. The dog seemed to instinctually know to be still.

It was a good ten minutes before the noise faded enough for her to feel like she could move. She rose to her feet. "Come on, girl. Let's go find your sister."

Betty followed her to where she'd stashed the ATV, which had a platform on the tailgate with metal sides, creating a sort of basket with a door, designed for Betty to travel in. Betty jumped up into her place and Catherine started up the ATV, got it turned around and headed toward the camp.

Her intent was to pick up a few supplies and hope that Liz would show up. Otherwise, she'd have to search for the other dog while avoiding the two ATV riders. Betty was trained to respond to different hand signals, commands and even a whistle. Catherine had no idea what commands Liz had been trained to respond to. The dog came when her name was called, but shouting might attract the wrong kind of attention. Betty waited in her carrier while Catherine quickly loaded some food, utensils and supplies to make a fire. She grabbed a canteen filled with water and placed the items in the saddle bags on the ATV, giving Betty's head a quick pet.

The hum of an ATV told her she could no longer be in the open. She had just reached her ATV when the man in the helmet emerged through the trees headed straight toward her.

She hurried to get settled on the ATV as the man idled and reached inside his jacket. She turned the key in the ignition.

The helmeted rider lifted his hand from inside his jacket without pulling the gun, knowing he was too far to get an accurate shot. He drove the ATV closer to her just as she rumbled toward the trees.

The second rider, the man with the blue eyes, emerged from the forest.

Catherine did a double take. Liz was sitting on the front of the seat nestled in the rider's unzipped jacket. Why would the dog trust a stranger?

After the blue-eyed rider lifted his leather jacket and Liz jumped from the ATV, he moved toward the man whose face was hidden by a helmet, cutting the other rider off with his ATV before he got close enough to fire an accurate shot at Catherine.

The helmeted rider lifted his gun, but the blue-eyed man was already on top of him pulling him off the ATV. Why was the blue-eyed man protecting her?

Catherine was grateful that neither man had had time to fire a shot. It could have sent Liz into the forest again.

"Liz, come!" Catherine called.

The dog spotted her and headed her way. Catherine got off the ATV and boosted Liz up into the carrier where Betty greeted her by licking her face.

While the two men were fighting, she had a chance to get away.

Catherine jumped on the four-wheeler and twisted the throttle. As she headed toward the forest, she couldn't shake an uneasy feeling. Liz had trusted the man with the blue eyes enough to get on the ATV with him, and he had stopped the other man from shooting her.

Maybe the two men weren't working together after all. None of it made sense. All she knew was that two men with guns was bad news. She still needed to focus on her own survival and getting the dogs to safety.

As she headed toward the trail that was a long ride back to her cabin and beyond that, the little town of Two Bits, she prayed she would get enough of a head start that the men wouldn't see where she went and she could get back to civilization alive.

When she looked at the gas gauge, she saw that she was low on fuel. Tension threaded through her chest. Now escape was going to be even harder.

THREE

Ryan sought only to subdue the helmeted rider. His focus was on catching Victoria before she got away. He landed a blow to the man's stomach and then his back, which put the man on his knees. The helmet protected his head.

Though his ankle still hurt, Ryan ran back to his vehicle, jumped on and headed in the direction he'd seen Victoria go.

He could hear her ATV as he followed her on the trail through the forest, but he could not see her.

The evergreens opened up into a meadow, and he spotted the glow of the other vehicle's taillights as it rumbled toward a stand of trees.

He revved the engine and rolled across the grass wondering how he could possibly catch up to her without risking a wreck. At least the grass of the meadow was less slippery than the muddy trails, and the incline more gradual than the trail that had brought him to this remote location.

The route through the meadow wasn't even really a trail. He wondered where Victoria was going.

He glanced over his shoulder, knowing that the other rider would recover and probably follow him. He needed to get to Victoria before the helmeted rider got to him.

He pressed the gas and watched the speedometer move as he rolled toward the trees where Victoria had gone. Once in the forest, there was a wide trail clearly used for vehicles like his. The trees ended, and he came out on a trail that had a steep drop-off on one side and a mountain on the other.

He kept going, aware that one slip could send him rolling down the mountain. Gradually, the incline leveled off and there were some trees down below instead of a rocky death trap.

When he'd gone for at least another ten minutes without seeing the other ATV, he began to wonder where Victoria was. He had a view of sections of the trail as it wound down the mountain. He stopped and let the ATV idle, watching for any sign of her below but seeing only forest, rocks and trail. It didn't seem like she'd gone this way. She must have veered off somewhere.

When he turned his machine off, he could hear nothing but forest sounds and the soft drizzle of the rain. He'd not had time to put his helmet back on. His hair was soaked.

She had to have gone off the trail where the land leveled off. Probably hiding somewhere or maybe she took a connecting trail by going cross-country. After he found a wide spot in the road, he turned around. Fully aware that he ran the risk of encountering the helmeted rider, he eased back along the trail much more slowly until he saw the indentation of tracks that led off the main trail. That had to be where she'd gone.

He turned the handlebars and followed the tracks until they were no longer clearly marked. He got off his vehicle and checked the ground more closely for indentations.

The hum of a motor up on the trail told him that the helmeted rider had just sped by. Would he keep going or would he backtrack as well?

Ryan and the ATV were mostly hidden from the other rider by some brush. Still, he couldn't waste time. He thought he saw the glint of metal through the trees, a parked ATV maybe?

He had to find her. If he approached on foot, she wouldn't hear him coming.

He kept walking, seeing a fresh tire track now and then that told him he was headed in the right direction. He came to her ATV covered in pine boughs to hide it from view.

It appeared her strategy was to hide until she thought both he and the other rider were far enough away that she could make a safe escape probably on another trail. She seemed to have solid knowledge of the trail system and she likely had a plan.

But why hide, why not just try to get away?

He noticed the gas gauge on her ATV. When he turned the key in the ignition, the needle showed it was one line away from empty. She didn't have enough gas to get out of here. There had been gas cans at the camp. She probably planned on returning before escaping. No wonder she needed to wait him and the other guy out.

He looked all around the area, hoping to see a footprint that might tell him which direction she'd gone. It was a distant single yip of a dog that told him which way he needed to walk.

He moved through the trees, stopping to listen. He heard her talking soothingly to the dogs before he saw her. He stepped quietly toward the sound of her voice, grateful that the rain masked his footsteps.

She and the dogs had taken refuge in a lean-to built from pine boughs and covered in a weathered tarp, which indicated it must have been there for a while.

He stepped out into the open raising his hands in surrender, knowing that seeing his gun had frightened her.

Her head shot up. The wide eyes and the hardness of her features indicated fear.

"I'm not here to hurt you," said Ryan.

Liz wagged her tail at the sound of his voice.

"Whatever you've done, Victoria, we might be able to work something out," he said.

She rose to her feet and squared her shoulders. "Victoria? What are you talking about?"

Fear struck through Catherine at the sight of the man with the blue eyes. Betty growled at her feet, taking up a protective stance incongruent with Liz's wagging tail. Dogs were a good judge of character, but she was getting a very mixed message from the collies.

It seemed this man thought she was Victoria. "What's going on here? Why do you think I'm my twin sister?"

The man dropped his hands to his sides as his face drooped. She watched him closely. He would have to unzip the jacket to get to the gun.

His forehead wrinkled in confusion. "Twin? We didn't have a lot of personal conversations, but it seems like Victoria would have mentioned having an identical twin sister."

"Long story," said Catherine. "But my sister and I were not on the best of terms before she disappeared." This man had known Victoria. Why did it hurt that her sister hadn't mentioned her to him?

The man shook his head. "I'm not sure what brought you to this point to be hiding up here. But the bureau will work with you."

He didn't believe that she wasn't Victoria. "I honestly don't know what you're talking about."

Liz kept wagging her tail and whimpering. The man

with the blue eyes kneeled down. "Hey there, Liz." His hair was slicked back from the rain, revealing a firm jawline.

The dog ran to him bouncing around and licking his face. There was something sweet about the way he interacted with Liz.

"She knows you?"

"Yes, but you know that, right? You brought her with you when we would meet in the park."

"I am *not* Victoria. My name is Catherine."

"Okay." The tone of his voice suggested he still didn't believe her. "Do you want to explain to me why your sister wouldn't have talked about you?"

"Our parents split when we were thirteen. She chose to live with mom in the city, and I stayed on the family farm with our father. It was an unhappy marriage and a bitter divorce. We were always sort of opposites, but when we were forced to choose sides, it caused a chasm between us."

There were more reasons for the lack of communication. Four years ago, when she'd gotten engaged, Catherine had tried a reconciliation traveling to Seattle with her fiancé. Only to have Victoria steal her fiancé and then dump him months later. The marriage to Dave had been a sort of rebound. He had said all the right things and seemed to offer a refuge to the betrayal and loss. But his promises and the picture he painted of their life together had all been lies that had created an even worse nightmare for her.

On the road above them, she could hear the put-put of the engine of the other ATV as the helmeted rider went by. The rider had turned back around and was searching for her.

The blue-eyed man angled slightly toward the sound, though the road was not visible through the trees.

Fear struck through her. The noise was a reminder that another threat was out there. "Who is that guy, anyway?"

"I think he might be looking for some diamonds Victoria may have taken, and he might want revenge on her for the theft."

"You mean…he wants to kill her." What if the helmeted rider thought she was Victoria as well?

"Look, Catherine, or whoever you say you are." The tone of his voice indicated he still wasn't buying her story. "My name is Ryan McCloud. I'm an FBI agent. Victoria was working with us to track down the players in an international jewelry smuggling ring." He unzipped his jacket.

Holding her hand up, she took a step toward him even as her heart raced. "Oh no, you don't. I know you have a gun."

"I was going to show you my badge." His voice took on a gentle, almost sympathetic quality.

She shook her head, still unwilling to trust what he was saying.

"I promise I won't touch the gun. I'll open up my jacket real slow." He unzipped his jacket all the way and turned it so she could see the lining. "I'll just be reaching into this interior pocket."

The PTSD that being with Dave had caused meant that any sense that violence might erupt made her on edge and hypervigilant. Her hands were shaking. Betty whimpered in response to her agitated state.

Ryan reached into an interior pocket and pulled out a badge and ID. The sight of the badge made her twitch. Dave had been a police officer. "I noticed that you are low on gas. You don't have enough to get off this mountain. I'll go back with you to the camp to get gas. That is your plan, right? That is why you hid here?"

He was offering protection. He had already saved her once from the other rider. "Okay, you can come with me to get the gas." But she still wasn't sure if she could trust him. "And then I will go down this mountain by myself."

"I can't get out of here on my own. It's clear you know all the shortcuts and back trails. That man is after me as much as he's after you. Right now, we need each other."

She was pretty sure that Ryan still thought she was Victoria. If Victoria had stolen diamonds, she probably would be under arrest if she ever surfaced. Did Ryan intend to take her in until she could prove who she was? She had no ID on her. There was no need for it up here. Although an ID would be easy enough to fake. She wondered if she had any pictures of her sister and herself together back at the cabin. Certainly, there were none of them together as adults. Maybe if she had proof that she was a twin he would believe her.

His words, *right now we need each other*, echoed through her head. After Victoria and her fiancé's betrayal and Dave's abuse, she'd decided that all she needed was herself, her dog and God. This situation with Ryan was temporary. She did need some protection to get the gas. Liz seemed to like him. As long as he thought she was Victoria, he'd want her alive.

She swept past him, stopping briefly to meet his gaze.

"Try and keep up." She sought to make her voice sound strong despite feeling like jelly inside. She called the dogs and hurried toward where she'd camouflaged her ATV. Thinking he was reaching for his gun had left her shaken. She wasn't sure her mind or body could take even the threat of violence after what she'd been through in her marriage.

He ran past her, and she saw then where he had parked his vehicle not far from hers. The helmeted rider must not have glanced down here. That didn't mean he wouldn't find them once they were out in the open.

Despite Ryan's offer of help, her life was still under threat.

FOUR

Once they were both on their ATVs, the woman who said her name was Catherine zoomed out ahead of him. She had far more skill on these machines than he did. Her admonition to keep up with her had been sincere. She wasn't going to slow down and wait for him. And maybe that was her plan, to shake him.

It was clear she didn't trust him.

He still wasn't sure she wasn't Victoria. Except for the hair style, which was easy enough to change, the mannerisms and way of speaking were pure Victoria. Was this part of Victoria's clever ruse to get away from him, to pretend like she didn't know him under the guise of the made-up twin story?

When he'd worked undercover as a jewelry merchant and tagged Victoria as a good candidate to turn into an informant, it was because she seemed to have a moral streak. At an international jewelry show, he had bought an emerald from her and overpaid cash on purpose. She'd caught the error, tracked him down and returned the money. Her desire for justice extended to not liking that the illegal trade had an unfair advantage. No informant was perfect, though. There were things about Victoria that were concerning as well. She had very expensive taste, and she had mentioned having debt.

Informants turned on agents all the time. No one knew that better than he did. On a prior assignment, he'd had an informant go back to the drug trade. Now with what had happened with Victoria, he wondered if he'd lost his ability to read people. He'd never been good at it in romantic relationships and now it seemed to be affecting his work.

Ryan certainly couldn't get any clear understanding on the woman who called herself Catherine. Who was she really? He'd encountered deception and betrayal in his job and now he didn't trust his own judgment.

He watched the dogs in their carrier as she swept up the hill and back on a trail headed in the opposite direction from where the other rider had gone. The two dogs balanced on the back tailgate with its meshed metal railing. They exhibited a high level of agility as they were shaken back and forth.

She took a sudden turn when they got to where the forest opened up into meadow. This was a different way than she'd gone before when she was leaving the camp.

He saw then that the new path sheltered them in the trees more. The camp came into view, and he realized the way she had taken him had gotten them back much faster and had kept them hidden from view.

She dismounted her four-wheeler and wandered the camp in search of the gas cans, glancing nervously toward the trees. He got off his vehicle and helped her with the search, finding one underneath a tarp. He handed her the gas can. She thanked him, unscrewed her cap on the tank, stuck the nozzle in and poured.

She was just twisting the cap on when the helmeted rider made his appearance at the edge of the trees. Not close enough to fire off an accurate shot, the man zoomed toward them. Ryan and Catherine jumped on their respective vehicles.

Catherine took a cross-country route that led her up the mountain. Though they were still headed in the same general direction, this was a different trail than he'd come in on. She seemed to know all the shortcuts.

The other rider gained on him.

He heard a loud popping noise and then the ATV bounced like it had square wheels. One of the tires had been shot out.

Ryan dismounted, pulled his gun and turned to shoot at the tires of the helmeted rider.

In response, the rider jerked his handlebars, whipping the vehicle out of the line of fire but causing it to tilt on its side. It would take him a few minutes to get upright.

Ryan glanced at his own defunct vehicle with the flat tire. Catherine idled up ahead and signaled with her hand that he should get on with her. So, she wasn't going to leave him stranded.

While the helmeted rider sought to get his ATV operational, Ryan ran to where Catherine waited for him. She scooted forward, and he squeezed into the tiny space between the dog carrier and her back. Her hair smelled like peaches as it brushed against his face.

Her ATV surged ahead. With a high level of skill, she worked her way up the hill around rocks and fallen logs. They weren't even on a trail.

When he looked over his shoulder, he saw that the other rider was still tailing them but had fallen behind.

Once at the top, she traveled cross country. Nothing looked familiar to him.

The rain pelted his neck where it was exposed. And he felt a chill sink into his bones. His ankle still ached.

Catherine steered the ATV through a stand of trees.

Though the rain continued to fall, the ground leveled off and they came to a dirt road.

This time when he glanced over his shoulder, he saw no sign of the other rider. She had managed to shake him.

Once on the road, she sped up. They must have traveled for at least a mile.

She stopped in front of a tiny cabin tucked back in the trees. He dismounted first and then she jumped off the ATV and opened the carrier for the dogs. They both jumped down.

Ryan glanced toward the cabin. "This is your place?"

"On loan from the forest service," she said. "We can get warmed up inside."

"What about the guy in the helmet?"

"I don't think he was able to follow me," she said. "We're both shivering and so are the dogs. You keep favoring your right foot."

He was cold. "All the same, we shouldn't stay here long."

"I'm pretty sure that guy won't be able to follow the way I went," she said.

"What's farther down the mountain?"

"A little town called Two Bits. The rider might go straight there," she said. "It's got to be where he rented his ATV, and he probably thinks that's where we'll go."

"Yes, that's where I rented my ATV. I'm just all turned around as to where I'm at." He wasn't sure why she was so insistent they stop. Maybe they had shaken the other rider, but why take a chance. Then again, going into Two Bits might not be safe either. She was right that the town would be the likely place to find them.

She reached underneath the stairs, pulling out a hide-a-key and unlocking the door. Inside, the place was one giant room—bed, couch and kitchenette. He assumed the closed door must be the bathroom. There was a woodstove with two overstuffed chairs by it.

Catherine worked quickly to get a fire started in the woodstove. She filled a kettle with water and placed it on top of the stove. She poured some water in the dogs' bowls, which they quickly lapped up.

Kneeling, Catherine patted the dogs' heads. He saw a softness in her when she interacted with the dogs that was endearing.

She looked at him. "Take your jacket off and hang it over the chair close to the stove so it can dry out." The rain had soaked the part of his shirt that had been exposed. He was still nervous about being found, but he did as she instructed.

The dogs curled up in front of the stove.

She brought him an ice pack from the kitchen. "For your injured ankle."

He took it from her. His fingers brushed over hers causing heat to travel up his arm. "Thank you." Her touch had made his heart flutter. How unexpected. He placed the compress on his ankle. The pain wasn't as bad as it had been earlier, so he didn't think his ankle was broken, just twisted.

Catherine pulled a suitcase out from underneath the bed and opened it. Then she went to a satchel hanging on a coatrack and retrieved a wallet. She sat down in the plush chair beside him and handed him a license from the wallet and an unframed photograph that she had taken out of the suitcase.

The license identified her as Catherine Reed. The face that stared back at him could be Victoria's. IDs were easy enough to fake. The photo was of two teen girls with their arms around each other. A barn was visible in the background. Though one had short wavy hair and the other had two long braids, the facial features were identical, and both looked like younger versions of Victoria. The photo would be harder to fake, and why would she have something like that readily available.

"I'm not Victoria. Can we please put your suspicion to rest?"

So that was her motive in stopping here. She was very good at reading people and had picked up on the fact that he still hadn't given up on her being Victoria.

"Okay, I believe the twin story now." His spirits sank. That meant his efforts to find his informant had been in vain, and now he'd dragged Catherine into this mess.

He stared at the license. "You have a different last name than Victoria."

"I was married."

"Was?"

"I don't want to talk about it." She jerked to her feet and towered over him. "Look, I don't know what Victoria got herself into, but it doesn't concern me. I'll give you a ride into town and that will be the end of it. Betty and I need to get back to work."

He wasn't so sure about that. The man chasing them thought she was Victoria. He couldn't begin to imagine who the rider was working for. The mafia, who had a heavy hand in the illegal diamond trade? Or the mystery man also engaged in the trade and trying to take over mafia turf? "What went on between the two of you that your sister wouldn't mention you?"

A pained look came across her face. "Just a lot of water under the bridge. My sister and I became two very different people." She sat back down in the chair and stared at the fire. "I can tell you one thing. I know what the official report said about Victoria. Missing...presumed dead." She turned to face him. "My sister is not dead."

"And how do you know that?"

"Some bonds can't be broken no matter what has happened between us. She's alive." She touched her hand to her heart "I feel it right here."

It was nice to have his gut instinct confirmed. "How did you end up with her dog?"

"Mom never took to country life and being on a farm, and Victoria adopted the same attitude. I think we chose sides before the divorce ever happened. The one thing Victoria loved about the farm was the dogs. After Dad died, there was no more breeding and training operation. I leased out the farm. Liz and Betty are the last in the line."

Both dogs raised their heads at the sound of their names. The kettle on the stove whistled. Catherine rose and lifted it. "You want some hot cocoa?"

"I don't think there is time for that. We should get moving." At the very least, he needed to go back to town and get his car and explain to the rental place what had happened to the ATV, even if it meant another encounter. The heat from the stove was relaxing, but he knew he couldn't let his guard down.

"Okay," she said.

"You still haven't said how you ended up with Liz. We had Victoria's place under surveillance from the time we realized she was missing."

"Victoria and I had an agreement that if anything ever happened to one of us, the other would make sure the dog was okay."

"Now that I think about it, we assumed she had taken the dog with her. She clearly loved Liz," said Ryan.

"Victoria left the dog with a friend who called me when Victoria didn't return when she said she would. This was even before her boss at the jewelry store filed a missing person's report."

It seemed Victoria had made arrangements to make sure the dog was taken care of. More evidence that her disappearance was planned.

Catherine looked directly at Ryan. Her features grew tight and her brow furrowed. "What has my sister done?"

"I don't know. She may have taken a large amount of diamonds. She could have decided it was more lucrative to work for the gem smugglers. There is more than one player in this illegal trade, and right now there is a turf war, one side backed by the mafia. She may have been outed as an informant and feared for her life. Though, if that was the case, I don't know why she wouldn't have come to me. The bureau could have protected her."

She shook her head, biting her lower lip. "I'm not sure what my sister could have done. We grew apart, and she changed so much. I do know appearances and material things were always important to her, I just can't picture her deciding to throw in with criminals."

"Maybe she had no choice," said Ryan. "She could have been coerced. I won't know anything until I find her." With his lead in Montana coming to a dead end, he wasn't sure what his next move was to find Victoria. He knew he had to make sure that Catherine wasn't in danger first.

"Was she in financial trouble?" She stood up and ran her fingers through her hair.

"She mentioned having some debt. Maybe it was worse than she let on. Still, taking the diamonds from smugglers seems a little high risk. She could've just pocketed a gem here and a gem there. Unless she was desperate and in a hurry."

Catherine crossed her arms and paced. "Like you said, we should get going into town. I'll drop you off."

"And what? You're just going to go back to work in the

middle of nowhere by yourself? Look, that guy up on that mountain thinks you're Victoria."

Fear flashed across her face. "Are you saying he's going to try to come after me again?"

"I'm just saying Victoria made a lot of really bad people angry when she and the diamonds disappeared."

Her hand fluttered to her chest. "That has nothing to do with me." Her voice faltered as she spoke.

"Maybe you shouldn't ditch me so fast," said Ryan. "I may have brought trouble to your door and for that I'm sorry. I feel an obligation to make sure you're safe."

Catherine did not want to believe what she was hearing. "Betty and I have work to do. I'm not going to hole up in some safe house. I'll just let the sheriff know about the man on the four-wheeler. I'm in touch with forest service people who can also watch out for me." The wilderness was still the best hiding place from her ex-husband, and that was foremost on her mind.

She could feel her muscles tense as she grew more upset by the second. How was it that her sister could rip her life to pieces without even being in it?

"I'm not so sure that's a viable solution," said Ryan.

"But you don't know for sure if he'll come after me. I took such a zigzag route to this cabin, I don't think he'll find me here." Her thoughts raced as she tried to comprehend what to do. Maybe she was safe at the cabin, but the helmeted rider knew where her camp in the wilderness was. She would have to set up somewhere else. Her research took her all over the mountain.

"But you are not staying at the cabin, right?"

She saw how impossible the situation was. Still, the last thing she would ever trust was protection from a law enforcement officer. Hadn't Dave promised her that? She could figure this out alone. "Look, I'll take you into town and I'll deal with things on my own terms. I can take care of myself." She'd said that a lot since going into hiding from her ex. Who else could she depend on besides God?

"I don't think being alone is a good idea right now." Ryan turned toward the front window. His shoulders tensed, riding up toward his ears when he peered out. He whirled around. "Get down." He wrapped an arm around her back and took her to the floor. She felt the weight of his arm on her back.

Betty rose from where she rested and barked. Liz paced.

The front window shattered, spraying glass across the wood floor.

"He found us!" said Ryan.

His words reverberated in her brain, not sinking in. No, it couldn't be.

He rolled away from her and got to his feet. "The man on the ATV is here."

She moved to get up, comprehending the danger outside.

The guy had some tracking skills. She wasn't safe here or on the mountain. Though the cabin was partially hidden by trees, the ATV with its distinct dog carrier was parked outside. Denial still swirled through her thoughts. This could not be happening. The safe world she'd created was being ripped away from her.

"My car is parked on the side of the cabin," she said. "There's a back door." She called the dogs to her.

"Stay low." Ryan pulled his gun from its holster as a second shot rang out.

She grabbed her satchel where she'd set it down after tossing the wallet back in and crawled toward the back door. Ryan rose and fired a shot through the window.

The dogs remained close to her as she reached up to turn the doorknob. Another shot was fired, causing her to cringe. She swung the door open and rushed outside, still crouching. Once at the backside of the cabin, she stood up and ushered the dogs around the corner to where her car was parked. She opened the back door so they could jump in.

When she was behind the wheel, she dug for her car keys in the satchel and started the car. She stared through the windshield. The cabin was angled so the car wasn't visible from the front of the house.

Where was Ryan? How long should she wait?

If he was shot, it was just a matter of time before the helmeted rider went through the house, out the back door and found her.

She took in a jagged breath.

Ryan appeared at the passenger door and got in. "Go. He's in the cabin right now."

She hit the gas. In the rearview mirror, she saw the helmeted rider just as he came around the back of the cabin and raised his gun.

She sped toward the dirt driveway and out on the road with the man running after her, gun raised. A shot pinged off something.

The dirt road was single lane with trees lining both sides. She gripped the wheel and pressed the accelerator, going as fast as she dared.

Ryan glanced through the back window. "Keep going. He might try to follow us down."

"This car can go faster than his ATV." Her heart pounded as she tried to get a deep breath. She focused on the road ahead, not daring to check the rearview mirror.

Ryan glanced over his shoulder. "He's behind us on his ATV. Doesn't this car go any faster?"

The road was still muddy from the rain. "Not in these conditions."

She maneuvered around several tight curves. When she checked her mirrors, she couldn't see the man on the ATV anymore. She drove for several more minutes.

The road leveled off, and she breathed a sigh of relief when she saw the first house that indicated she was getting close to the little town of Two Bits. They passed a farm and more houses on the outskirts of town. She could see the cluster of buildings that bordered Main Street up ahead.

The town only had a couple hundred people and was largely a hub for hunters, hikers and ATVers to get supplies before they headed into the deep wilderness.

"Now what?"

"I don't see him anywhere," said Ryan. "Hard to believe he'd give up. Maybe he realized he couldn't catch us on the ATV. I don't think we've seen the last of him, though. Look how tenacious he was in finding that cabin."

Her mind was spinning. Her personal possessions were still at the cabin. She couldn't go back, not alone anyway. "This isn't the county seat. The sheriff's office is forty miles from here. I can get in touch with my forest service contacts, though."

"I think you're going to need more protection than that."

"What about my work?" Even as she objected, she knew that Ryan was right.

Ryan looked out the window and then at her. "Isn't it clear, it's not safe for you to go back up there alone?"

"I see that now." Her voice was barely a whisper. The idea that she would be dependent on Ryan for help and protection did not sit well with her.

The outdoors had always felt like the safest place to her. She could take a deep breath believing that her job kept her hidden from Dave being able to find her. And now something she had no control over had shattered her sense of peace. "Just like that, my whole life is ripped from me because of Victoria."

She found her resistance giving way to Ryan's logic. The attack at the cabin had proven the helmeted rider wasn't just going to call it a day. Her voice grew soft and she felt a tightness in her chest. "So what happens now?"

"Let me make some calls. See what I can do. I'm going to need to enlist some help from other agents in the nearest field office."

"I need to go back up to my cabin and get my things," she said.

"I'll see if I can make that happen only if we are sure we're not going to have another encounter. In the meantime, I have to talk to the outfit I rented the ATV from and let them know why I can't return it."

If Catherine wasn't going to be able to work and had to leave the area, she needed to tie up loose ends. "I need to inform the forest ranger who is my contact that I won't be able to work. I can do that with a phone call. I'd like to pick up my mail."

Coming up with the to-do list calmed the turmoil inside, giving her something concrete to focus on.

"I'll stay with you," said Ryan. "You shouldn't be out in the open alone."

She realized that Ryan must think the helmeted rider would follow them into town. Being close to Ryan ruffled her feathers. Perhaps it was because his demeanor reminded her of her ex-husband, whose protective behavior when they first met had been a façade to win her trust and make her open her heart to him. She had been too vulnerable. Never again.

"I can drive you to the ATV rental place after we get my mail."

"Lead the way," said Ryan.

She drove down what constituted Main Street, only four blocks of stores and an apartment building, and parked in front of the post office.

After cracking the window so the dogs could get air, she locked the car up. It was only a short walk to the post office. She glanced around and didn't see the man on the ATV anywhere. That didn't mean he wasn't hidden somewhere watching at a distance.

Other than Maude, the older woman who ran the post office, there was no one else inside the small room with its counter and wall of post office boxes.

"Hey there, Catherine. I thought you weren't coming down for supplies for more than a week." Maude watched Ryan with suspicion, narrowing her eyes at him.

The town was so small that any stranger was easily identified.

"Change of plans," said Catherine. The key to her post office box was on the same keychain as her car keys. She twisted the key and pulled out several envelopes.

She filed through them expecting to see only junk. She hesitated on a handwritten envelope. Her breath caught in her throat.

Ryan leaned toward her. "Everything okay?"

She touched the envelope with her finger. "This is my sister's handwriting."

FIVE

Ryan glanced at the gray-haired woman behind the counter, who seemed a little too interested in their conversation. "Let's go back to the car and have a look."

He tried not to get his hopes up. If this letter was genuine, it meant Victoria was alive and was trying to contact her sister.

Catherine's face had gone pale as she held the stack of mail. He guided her through the door and up the street. She gripped the keys in one hand and the mail in the other.

She still seemed to be in shock by the time they got to the car. "Why don't you drive?"

"Do you want to hand me the keys?" He took them from her hand when she opened it.

Once he unlocked the car, she skirted around to the passenger side.

He glanced up and down the quiet street, half expecting to see the helmeted rider. Maybe the guy had gone back to the rental place to get his car, in which case they wouldn't recognize him. They really couldn't stay in town much longer.

Once behind the wheel, he turned to face her. "You're sure that's your sister's handwriting?"

She nodded and touched the envelope again. "This is her distinctive right-leaning slant and the loops are more circles than ovals. We were homeschooled, so we practiced our penmanship together."

He leaned closer. The postmark was from twenty days after Victoria had been reported missing, which meant Catherine did not pick her mail up often. The return address was a PO box with no name. The sending address was marked *general delivery* with Catherine's name and the name of the town. "This isn't your permanent address, right?"

"I set up the PO box when I knew I would be working here long term." She took in a breath. "I don't have a permanent address anymore."

Doubt about Catherine clouded his mind. People who didn't want to be found for whatever reason chose not to have a permanent address. There was a lot he didn't know about this woman he was sitting next to. The truth was, with what had happened with his drug informant and now Victoria, he worried he had lost his ability to see people for who they really were.

He had initially not even trusted that Catherine was telling the truth about being a twin. And now it appeared that Catherine had a few secrets of her own.

He chose to focus on the issue at hand, knowing that Catherine had a lot to explain about how she chose to live, so isolated and unattached. "How would she have known to send the letter to this town?"

"Maybe from the friend who was taking care of Liz. I had to give her the name of the town where I was staying in order for Liz to get here safely." Catherine flipped the envelope open and tore at the seam. There was a single piece of paper inside with the same slanted handwriting.

Help me...no police.

Catherine closed her eyes.

His spirits lifted. Victoria was alive. Or at least she had been at the time the letter was sent. He had to believe she was out there and that the trail had not come to a dead end. He still might be able to bring her in with Catherine's help.

Catherine's fingers trembled.

He brushed his hand over hers, feeling the silky smoothness of her skin. "Hey. I know this is a shock."

She pulled away and scooted an inch toward the door, holding the letter close to her chest. "Why does she say no police?" Suspicion clouded her words.

"You can't think that the *no police* instruction is a reference to me." He was struggling with enough doubt. He didn't like the way she cast shade on who he was as an agent.

"You said it yourself. Why didn't she come to you for help if she was fearful about something?"

Catherine acted like she didn't trust him and now the chasm seemed to have widened. "Working with an informant is always a dicey thing. I don't know why she didn't come to me for help if she was in trouble."

"Do you think she took those diamonds?"

"I can't answer any of those questions until I find your sister," said Ryan. "She reached out to you. I thought you said things weren't that great between you."

"There's a lot of history between my sister and me, some of it not good." Catherine stared out the window for a long moment before turning back to meet his gaze. "That doesn't mean there isn't a bond between us. You said she never mentioned having a twin. Maybe she didn't tell other people either. If someone is after her, she couldn't go to anyone in her circle where she lived in Seattle. I might be her only option."

"The message doesn't say how to contact her," said Ryan.

Light flashed in Catherine's eyes. She knew something she wasn't telling him.

"Look, Catherine, we've got to work together on this. You want to find your sister and so do I. You need to tell me what you know."

She stared at the letter. "I'm not sure what to think, Ryan. Let's focus on the next thing we need to do. If I can't go back to work, I need to make some calls. Then I want to go back to my cabin and load up my things."

He knew better than to press her for answers. Best to try to build some trust with her first. "Only if I go up there with you."

"Okay, if that's how it has to be." Her response was frosty.

She must realize the danger she was in but was still reluctant to take his help. Victoria's "no police" comment had made things worse.

"First, while we are in town, I need to go pay up the ATV rental place. I'll probably have to pay a towing fee or something and for the damage to the tire. Guess I can leave my car there for now."

They drove to the edge of town where the ATV rental shop was connected to a gas station/convenience store. The store clerk was also the man who handled the rentals. Much of the advertisements and merchandise was geared toward hunters and backpackers.

While he settled up with the rental place, Catherine remained in the car talking on her phone, he assumed to the people who had hired her. He could see her through the large windows of the convenience store.

So far, he had seen nothing of the helmeted rider. Other than the man's muscular build, he didn't know what he looked like so he couldn't even ask the clerk if the man had come back there. It wasn't good to leave Catherine alone in the car with the dogs. He paid up and hurried outside.

He had some calls to make as well to his supervisor as to how to move forward with the investigation. The note indicated that the only person Victoria would come out of hiding for was Catherine, yet that could put her in danger. He wasn't sure how to proceed.

"You ready to go?" he asked.

"Sure, you can drive if you want."

At least she trusted him enough for that.

Before he started the car, Catherine turned toward the back seat and talked to the dogs. "Just hang in there. You're doing great." She reached back to pet them.

He drove toward the edge of town and back toward the road that led to the cabin wondering why they hadn't seen the helmeted rider and thinking it was just a matter of time before he made another appearance.

As they headed to the cabin to get her few possessions, Catherine's thoughts were a jumbled mess. Because of the "no police" comment, she hadn't wanted to tell Ryan that she knew where her sister was. Then again, if Victoria had taken the diamonds, maybe that was why she didn't want contact with law enforcement. She just did not know her sister well enough anymore to be sure of her motives.

The town the PO box was in was close to the family farm, indicating Victoria had returned to her childhood home.

Catherine had leased the place out, knowing she couldn't return once Dave made his threats. Though he lived ten miles away, friends in town had told her they'd seen him driving around. Dave was so tight with the other police officers in the county, none believed her about the death threats. Dave had used his position and charm to fool many people and tell lies about her.

She couldn't go back there alone, but trusting Ryan seemed foolhardy as well. She really didn't know him.

And yet, her sister needed her. Even that realization was rife with emotional turmoil. She had prayed that she could come to a place of forgiveness toward her sister taking the man she loved just for the sport of it. It didn't say much about her fiancé that he was so easily lured from her.

She prayed silently.

God, I need some guidance.

Ryan got to the edge of town and kept driving until they were on the dirt road that led to the cabin.

She came to a decision.

The conflicted emotions were not what mattered. She was the only one who could help Victoria. If her sister needed her, she had to put her hurt feelings aside.

They arrived at the cabin.

"You stay in the car for a minute. Keep the door locked." Ryan pulled his gun out. "Let me make sure that guy is not around before we go inside. Then we should probably hurry."

He clearly thought the threat was still out there. But just because they hadn't seen him in town didn't mean he wasn't in Two Bits.

With his gun drawn, Ryan circled the exterior of the cabin and then went inside. He stepped out on the porch and motioned for her to get out.

After letting the dogs out so they could stretch and pee, she ran up the stairs.

"I have to warn you," said Ryan. "It's a mess in there."

There hadn't been time to lock the door. She pushed it open. What she saw shouldn't have surprised her, but it did. The place had been ransacked.

Her stomach knotted up when she stared at the chaos. "He was looking for the diamonds?"

Ryan peered in. "Looks like it. That explains why we didn't see him in town. He probably figured he couldn't catch us on the ATV and turned around to search this place."

"I can't leave the cabin in this state. It's on loan from the forest service."

"I'll help you straighten up," Ryan said.

"Let me grab my things and set them aside." Though there wasn't much to rifle through, the condition of the cabin was disconcerting. Her suitcase had been pulled from underneath the bed and its contents spread across the floor. She gathered the clothes and other personal items, including the picture of her and Victoria.

Ryan worked to put things back in the kitchen cupboards.

The dogs wandered in through the open door. Betty sniffed a coat that had been flung to the floor then moved around the room smelling other items. Having anything out of place often unnerved the dog, who had strong powers of observation.

She rose to shut the door and peered out the broken window. "Do you think he's out there watching the cabin? That's why he didn't come after us in town." Liz came and sat by her feet. At least, the dogs would alert her if someone was close by.

Ryan placed a rinsed coffee mug in the dish rack. "I'm not sure what his plan is. The smart thing is not to stay here long just in case."

It seemed like if the helmeted rider was around, he would have come after them by now. He would have no way of knowing they would come back here.

She found her sleeping bag in the corner of the room where it had been ripped open with a knife. Down feathers were scattered across the floor. If there had been any doubt the man was searching for the diamonds, this clinched the theory. She pointed at the feathers. "I don't know how I'm going to clean this up."

She got a plastic bag from the kitchen and gathered as much of the mess up as she could, sweeping the remaining feathers into the bag.

Ryan was finished up in the kitchen and was sweeping the broken glass from the window when she hurried into the bathroom to grab the few personal items she kept there. She gathered the dogs' food and dishes and set everything by the door. "I'm ready to go." She met his gaze.

"Just where are we going to?" He wiped his hands on a towel, hung it on the stove handle and walked toward her. "Are you ready to tell me where your sister is?"

The angst she'd felt earlier returned. "She said no police. I can't go by myself, though. It's not just the man who came after me at the camp. The reasons are…complicated." Going back to the farm meant she was that much closer to where Dave lived.

"Is it a long drive? Maybe you can explain to me on the way there."

She had a decision to make. Could she trust Ryan enough to at least protect her from her ex-husband? Ryan was the one who had brought this new threat of violence into her life. The bottom line? She felt compelled to help her sister, and she couldn't do it alone. "What if Victoria sees you and it scares her away?"

"Why don't we cross that bridge when we get to it?" Ryan ran his fingers through his sandy-colored hair, then looked at her, his blue eyes probing. "I never gave her a reason not to trust me. If she thinks I'm out to hurt her, it's because she believed a lie someone else told her or she took the diamonds and knows I'll have to report that." He seemed upset at Victoria's expressed distrust of him.

Catherine took in a breath. She wanted to believe him. "The PO box where she sent the letter from is in a little town called Lewisville that is not too far from the family farm. That's probably where she is."

"You own a farm?"

"Yes, my sister and I inherited it when our dad died."

"You think she might actually be staying at the farm?"

Catherine shrugged. "Maybe. The people leasing the place are locals who would have known Victoria when we were growing up before she left with mom when she was a teenager. She might just be staying in the town too."

"So that's where we go? I don't want you to drive alone. I'll have to come back for my car. It's still at the rental place."

"Before we leave, there is something you need to know." Her throat constricted. It was hard to talk about the reasons behind her failed marriage. She always felt like she should have seen the red flags, not been so foolish as to believe Dave's lies. She thought that anyone she told would find her at fault for having been gullible.

"I'm listening." Ryan's voice grew softer.

"I have an ex-husband who has vowed to kill me if he finds me. He lives not too far from where I think my sister is hiding out."

He answered without hesitation."I can handle that."

The warmth in his voice and the confidence he expressed helped her feel reassured that telling him had been the right decision. She found herself being drawn to a man who could show such strength and compassion at the same time.

"I'd like to make some phone calls, maybe get some backup," he said.

"That would make things worse. If she sees a bunch of

FBI agents, for sure she won't come out of hiding to tell me what is going on. It's a risk for even you to come with me."

"I need to at least call my supervisor and tell him what's going on and get some direction from him. I can't go into this alone. That's against protocol."

"Okay, make the calls you need to make, but when it comes down to it, I don't want to scare my sister away. I'll drive so you can talk on the phone."

Ryan helped her load up her few possessions into the trunk. She opened the back door for the dogs then surveyed the forest that surrounded the little cabin that had been her home.

The man who thought she was Victoria was still out there.

As she sat behind the wheel, the weight of the potential violence that surrounded her made it hard to get a breath.

SIX

While Catherine drove, Ryan stared out at the country road. Catherine had trusted him enough to tell him about the danger her ex-husband posed. He could tell from the waver in her voice it hadn't been easy to let him know. She had shown such courage. He vowed he would keep her safe from that man.

A sign indicating that Two Bits was up ahead came into view. "It looks like we have to go back through Two Bits to get to where we're going?"

"Yes," said Catherine. "It's the only road to Lewisville."

The helmeted rider knew what they were driving. He might be in town looking for them since he hadn't made a second appearance at the cabin.

She came to the edge of town, slowing down as she eased onto Main Street.

Ryan kept an eye on the traffic behind them as well as looking at cars parked on the street and the people on the sidewalk. Even though he had no idea what kind of car he was looking for or what the man looked like, only that he had a muscular build, he was still on high alert. Anyone who stared at her car with too much interest would be suspect. "How long before we get to Lewisville?"

"It's about a two-hour drive," said Catherine.

He had already called his supervisor in Seattle to let him know the situation. If needed, he could get help from agents in a local field office, the closest of which was Bozeman. He'd gotten in touch to advise them of the situation. They had promised to provide as much support for his investigation as they could.

"How big is this town by your family farm?" Ryan glanced at the dogs in the back seat. Both were resting. They lifted their heads when he looked at them.

"Less than a thousand people," she said. "Why?"

"Just trying to get a feel for what we are headed into." Agents were pretty good at blending in, but in a town that small, strangers would be noticed. Word might get back to Victoria before Catherine had a chance to make contact if other agents showed up. Right now, it would be best not to bring other agents to Lewisville.

Though he did not know why she'd said *no police*, he didn't want to scare Victoria away. It was Catherine she trusted, so it was Catherine who had to take the risk. He'd have to find a way to ensure her safety without frightening Victoria.

Catherine slowed down as the road became curvier.

It might help him to make decisions if he understood the dynamics of the sisters' relationship better. "You're taking a big chance to help your sister, even though it sounds like you were not on the best of terms."

Her jaw grew tight. "Family is family. That's what my dad always used to say. No matter what, she's still my sister. Really, she's the only close relative I have left."

Tension seemed to fill the car, and he thought it best not to probe more about Catherine's relationship with her twin.

Still, he needed to assess what he was getting himself into. "You want to tell me about this ex-husband? You think he'll come after you? I'm not trying to pry. I just need to know what I'm facing."

She flexed her hands on the steering wheel and then gripped it as her arms stiffened. "He lives about ten miles from town. If word gets to him that I'm around, he'll probably show up sooner or later." Her voice faltered.

"I can tell this isn't easy for you," he spoke gently.

"I just hope I can find Victoria quickly. Maybe we can get out of town before Dave shows up."

The more they talked, the more upset she became. So many aspects of her life were rife with pain. No more questions for now. A silence fell between them and he watched the road. He drew his attention to the car behind them. It had been there for some time, even though there were places it could have turned off.

"I see it too," she said. "Doesn't mean anything. Maybe he's just headed to the same place we are, right?"

"Could be. We'll just keep an eye on it. He hasn't tried anything." Catherine was risking so much by trying to make contact with her sister. He appreciated her bravery. "If there was any other way for me to track down Victoria, I would do it."

She drove staring straight ahead at the road. After several minutes, she let out a breath.

"You should know my ex-husband, Dave Reed, is a deputy with the county. He has a lot of influence on law enforcement in that area. All my complaints fell on deaf ears. The police took his side. It was just easier to leave. You need to know what you're up against if he does show up."

Now she seemed even more courageous for choosing to go to Lewisville. "No one would help you?"

"Not in that county. Dave can be a very charismatic and convincing man. It was more prudent to get a job that took me into the wilderness than try to press charges. Believe me, I tried everything. The restraining order really didn't make a difference. It just made him angrier."

Compassion for what she'd been through rose up. "You've been through some pretty bad stuff," he said. "You decided hiding in the mountains was the best solution?"

"I didn't think of it as hiding. I liked my job, actually. Both Betty and I were pretty happy."

"Kind of lonely," he said.

"I didn't mind it." Her voice held a note of sadness. "Just not the life I thought I would be living."

The car continued to follow them. He noticed a sign for a picnic area. "Why don't we pull over there? I want to see what this other car behind us does."

She hit her blinker. When she stopped, neither of them got out of the car right away. The other car, a tan sedan, slowed but rolled by on the road.

It didn't mean he wouldn't pull over and wait for them to get back on the road or come back around to get at them. Ryan felt the weight of his gun where it rested in the shoulder holster against his chest.

Liz whimpered from the back seat.

Catherine turned toward the dogs. "Is it okay to let them out or were you just seeing what that other driver would do?"

"I suppose the dogs have to stretch and pee anyway," he said.

Catherine unbuckled her seatbelt and got out. He unzipped his jacket to have easier access to his gun. She let the dogs out of the back seat.

Several cars whizzed by on the road. The dogs roamed around sniffing. She called them to her, petting them and talking sweetly. Victoria had the same demeanor when she interacted with Liz, a genuine connection between human and canine.

Catherine's face brightened when she interacted with the dogs. The look of permanent worry seemed to fade from her features. The sun, though low on the horizon, highlighted the gold strands in her auburn hair. He was struck by how pretty she was.

Catherine had many of the same mannerisms as her sister. Though as he was getting to know her, he realized she was a very different person from the somewhat prickly Victoria.

"Betty has training, but was Liz anything more than a pet?"

"I think Victoria at one point wanted to train her to sniff out gems, including diamonds."

"A dog can be taught that?"

She ruffled both animals' heads. "Border collies are smart. They can be taught almost anything."

Though Ryan was still concerned about an attack, he was glad the picnic site was visible from the road where a car went by every few seconds. Not likely someone would try something out in the open like this.

"You want to take over the driving duty since you're done with your phone calls?" She tossed him the keys. "Just stay on this road. It will take you right into Lewisville."

She loaded the dogs. They got in and he pulled out on the road. Within minutes, the tan sedan was behind them again. He hadn't tried to run them off the road. The guy hadn't tried anything, so Ryan couldn't even alert highway patrol to stop and question him.

It was clear, though, they were being followed. Maybe the driver was hoping they would lead him to the diamonds. Though he had no proof, it was probably the same man who had chased them on the ATV.

Catherine sat with her satchel in her lap twisting the strap around her hand. The quick glances in the mirror told him she saw the car too. "I think maybe we should go to the farm first. Find out if the people leasing it have heard or seen anything related to Victoria. It's a quick turn. Maybe we'll be able to ditch this guy."

"Sure, we can do that," he said. "If you think it would work."

"If this guy is able to follow us there, it would be pretty obvious that he's the guy who came after us in the mountains," she said.

"I'm not sure what his deal is. He hasn't tried anything." The terrain had changed from forest to more open farmland. "Let me know the way to the farm."

"In about twenty minutes, you'll make a right turn on an unmarked road." Clearly nervous, she ran her hands through her hair and bit her lower lip. "You have to turn before you get to the water tower. That's the only landmark. I'll let you know when we're getting close."

"If Victoria is there, it would be better if I stayed out of sight. I can hang back in the car while you talk to the people who live there and see if she is staying with them."

She nodded.

The rest of the drive went by quickly. "Up ahead is the turnoff," said Catherine. "It's a dirt road. See the water tower?"

"I see it," said Ryan.

The sedan still hung close behind them.

He waited until the last second to make the turn. Once again, the tan sedan whizzed by. Ryan slowed down on the dirt road but kept checking the mirror. Within minutes, a house and several barns came into view. "This is where you grew up?"

Her voice softened a little. "Yes, I loved it here."

Betty made a yipping sound from the back seat.

Catherine laughed and turned to talk to her dog. "You know this place, don't you?"

Betty responded with an enthusiastic bark.

Ryan rolled to a stop and didn't see any sign of people at the farmhouse. The place looked pretty isolated. It appeared the tan sedan hadn't turned around and followed them, but if Catherine had to wander the grounds alone, that would put her at risk.

He stared back at the road. "I suppose if anyone showed up, we'd see them coming." He had his gun. He was ready for a confrontation.

"I'm taking the dogs with me to knock on the front door," said Catherine.

He slid down in his seat so he wouldn't be immediately visible to someone staring out the window or walking the grounds. It would look like Catherine had come alone.

Catherine let out a breath and pushed open her door. "Hopefully, this will be easy. Victoria will be here, and she'll be tired of being in hiding."

Ryan watched as Catherine unloaded the dogs, who did gleeful circles around her and then sniffed every blade of grass. As she headed up the stairs to the farmhouse, he wondered what she would find out.

Catherine felt a tightening through her chest and stomach as a cavalcade of emotions hit her. She'd been forced to leave the place she loved because of Dave's threats. Would seeing Victoria bring up all the hurt she'd caused? As much as she loved the farm, coming back here was a reminder of all the loss she'd suffered.

She knocked on the door and waited, giving a backward

glance to where Ryan waited in the car. She could barely see his head above the dashboard. The dogs ran up on the porch and then back down. At least they were happy to be here.

"Catherine, what a nice surprise." Celeste, the wife of the man she'd leased the property to, came around a corner of the house. She wore gardening boots and held a hose. "What brings you to this neck of the woods? Wish I would have known you were coming. I'd have baked some muffins. I can put coffee on for you."

Celeste had lived in the Lewisville area for years and knew Catherine's whole family history. Her husband Ralph had been friends with Catherine's father.

"I don't have time for coffee, Celeste. I'm in kind of a serious situation. I'm wondering if Victoria showed up here."

Celeste shook her head. "I haven't run into her. I'd heard through the gossip mill that she was in town staying with Andrea York."

Andrea was their childhood piano teacher. Of course, that's where she would go. Andrea and Victoria had been very close at one time.

"Thank you." She headed down the steps. "Does Andrea still live in the same house?"

Celeste nodded. "You know things don't change much around here."

The dogs had run over to Celeste to be petted, wagging their tails so vigorously their behinds shook. Celeste pulled off her gardening gloves and kneeled to give the dogs some attention. "It was good to see you. Maybe you can come back some time and stay a while."

Not as long as her ex lived close by. "Maybe someday." Her throat went tight. Celeste knew about Dave's threats. Both she and her husband had been supportive. "Take care of yourself."

Celeste rose to her feet and stepped toward Catherine. "Is there anything I can do to help?"

She gave Celeste a quick hug. "Victoria may be in some trouble. I'm trying to get things straightened out."

She called the dogs and hurried back to the car. Once the dogs were loaded and she settled in, she spoke to Ryan. "She's in town staying with an old friend."

"Okay, I assume we head back up the road we just came in on?"

The tightness in her throat had not subsided and she could feel tears warming her eyes. "If we take the other exit from the farm, it will bring us out closer to town." She pointed in the direction they needed to go. And they would be less likely to encounter the tan sedan.

As Ryan backed out, she watched Celeste hooking up the hose and spraying a rosebush that Catherine's mother had planted years ago. Would there ever be a day when she could live at the place she loved so much?

"Everything okay?" The car rolled down the washboard dirt road.

"Just hard to come back here."

His voice filled with compassion. "Lot of emotions coming up?"

She swiped at her eyes before the tears had a chance to start flowing. "For sure."

Once they were back on paved road, Catherine gave Ryan the directions into town. They came to the outskirts where the grain silos were. "Andrea's house is by the school about five blocks from here and then a right turn, up two blocks."

Ryan passed the school and turned. "What does the house look like?"

"It's that red brick one right up there," she said.

He parked a block away.

"Here, give me your phone," said Ryan. "Let me put my number in it. If she is there, you can text me."

She pulled the phone from her satchel and handed it to him. "I don't know how else to do this." A cloud of suspicion hung over her sister.

"I'll still be close by." He handed her back the phone. "Just find out why Victoria wants to get in touch with you. I have to tell you that at some point, we will have to bring her in for questioning at the very least."

"I get that." Her stomach was in a tight knot. "Let's try to win her trust first."

Taking the dogs with her again, she walked the remaining distance and knocked on the door. She heard footsteps and the door swung open. It seemed to Catherine that Andrea had always had gray hair and was like someone's grandmother even when she was a kid. The older woman hadn't aged at all.

"Andrea?"

A stunned look crossed Andrea's face. Her mouth hung open.

"It's Catherine. You thought I was Victoria?"

"I thought she'd come back," said Andrea.

"Come back? Wasn't she staying with you?"

"Yes, but she saw a man across the street when we went to the grocery store, a stranger. Seemed to frighten her. She jumped in her car and left."

"Did she say where she was going or if she'd be back?"

Andrea shook her head. "I honestly don't know. She was really afraid." She turned to one side as if to provide Catherine with a view of the room. "She left her stuff here."

"How long ago was that?"

"Less than two hours ago."

She'd missed her sister by such a short time. If only she'd

checked her mail sooner. "Can I see what she left behind?" Maybe there would be some indication of where she would have gone in her things. She pulled her phone out to text Ryan.

She was here but is gone. She left her stuff.

He texted right back. I'd like to have a look at her personal possessions.

Ryan was thinking along the same lines as she was. Catherine turned to face Andrea. "Victoria may be in some trouble."

Andrea touched her mouth with her fingers. "Oh my, she didn't give any hint of that while she was here. Just said she wanted to get out of the rat race of the city. What kind of trouble?"

"I'm not sure. There's an FBI agent helping me find her. Is it okay if he comes in and looks at what Victoria left behind?"

Andrea nodded. "Sure, I want to help any way I can."

She sent Ryan a message.

Come on over.

A minute later, Ryan knocked on the door even though it was still partially open. Catherine introduced him to Andrea as he stepped into the living room. He showed his credentials.

"Andrea, I'm so sorry for this invasion of privacy, but it's very important that I find Victoria quickly," said Ryan.

Catherine turned toward Ryan. "Andrea said that Victoria left town in a hurry when she saw a man on the street, a stranger, not someone from around here."

"She didn't say where she was going or who the man was?"

Andrea shook her head. "She said that the man was dangerous and that she needed to get out of town. She was really frightened. She ran into the store that her car was parked behind. A second later, her car was racing up the street headed north. The man must not have realized it was her car. He kept watching the store and then crossed the street and went inside."

"What did he look like?"

"Maybe in his thirties. Tall and thin. Curly brown hair." The man who had chased them in the wilderness had been muscular. This sounded like a different man.

"Did Victoria say anything to you about what was going on in her life?"

"She just said she needed a break from her life in the city." Andrea tugged on her shirt collar. "She did seem jumpy, now that I think about it. I didn't want to pry. It was just good to see her after so many years."

"Let's have a look at what she left behind," said Ryan.

"Her stuff is in the guest room." Andrea turned toward a hallway.

They walked past a room that had a baby grand piano and down a hallway with the dogs following in single file. Andrea opened the door to a small room with a bed, nightstand and a chair by the window. An open suitcase lay on the bed.

Andrea stood at the door while Ryan stepped into the room. Catherine and the dogs stayed closer to the threshold.

Ryan moved toward the suitcase and carefully lifted each article of clothing.

"That's all she had was one suitcase?" Even that seemed uncharacteristic for Victoria, who could be a bit of a clotheshorse.

Andrea stepped into the room. "She had a smaller bag she must have put in the closet." She pulled a canvas bag slightly smaller than an airline carry-on from the floor of the closet and set it on the bed.

Ryan unzipped it. Inside was a bag filled with toiletries and a camera. At the bottom of the bag were two small zippered pouches. Ryan sat one on the bed and unzipped the other one. An object wrapped in a scarf was inside.

Catherine and the dogs stepped toward where Ryan unwrapped the object that was in the scarf.

Liz grew more agitated as Ryan unraveled the scarf. It seemed Victoria had taken some care in hiding and wrapping the object. Catherine wondered what it was.

Ryan unwrapped the last bit of the scarf. She leaned toward him to see what was hidden inside.

SEVEN

The object inside the scarf felt heavy in Ryan's hand. Liz made a whimpering sound when he lifted the final piece of the fabric. Inside was a small glass swan. The other scarf was wrapped around a glass horse. Neither looked particularly valuable or of high quality. They both looked like trinkets a person would buy in a tourist shop. Victoria had been in a hurry to get out of the city. Why take the time to grab something like this and conceal it?

"Are these family heirlooms or something?"

"I've never seen them before," said Catherine. "They look cheaply made."

Ryan left both objects on the bedspread and lifted the camera, which had only three digital pictures on it of three different glass vases. Victoria had a newfound fascination for glass objects. Ryan was struck by an idea. "You said Liz was trained to sniff out diamonds?"

Catherine nodded. "I think so."

Ryan picked up the glass horse and put it closer to Liz's nose. The dog sniffed, sat down and lifted her chin.

"That could be an alert," said Catherine. "Do you think there's a diamond hidden in there?"

Ryan looked closer at the horse. The glass was not smooth but had sort of a crackled quality. It was possible that it was a mixture of sugar and maybe some type of glue. Even when he held it to the light, there was nothing that visibly looked like a diamond. A clever way to smuggle the gems? The two glass miniatures were not large enough to hide the half million in diamonds that had disappeared.

"Why do you think my sister had those?" The nervous edge had crept back into her voice.

"Not sure." He didn't want to say. Someone on the run would need a money source. If the glass objects did conceal diamonds, that would have helped Victoria finance her escape. But she had left town without them. Then again, the pictures on the camera suggested that Victoria was gathering evidence of how the smuggling was taking place. "We'll take these in as evidence."

He went through the pockets of the larger suitcase. There were no notes or journals. "She had her purse with her when she bolted, nothing else?" He looked at Andrea, who nodded.

Victoria would have her phone and probably some money. Maybe ideas about where else she could hide were on her phone or on a note in her purse. There was nothing here to indicate where she may have gone.

Andrea tugged at her collar. "I wish I had known what was really going on with her."

Ryan pulled a business card from his pocket. "If she comes back or gets in touch with you, I need to be informed right away." He turned back toward the glass figurines. "I'll need to take these and the camera. Do you have plastic bags I could put them in?"

"Sure, in my kitchen," said Andrea.

They headed back down the hallway into the living room and then the kitchen, where Andrea pulled out two bags for Ryan.

"I can put the camera in my satchel," said Catherine. Ryan handed it to her.

They walked back into the living room. Andrea held the door for them while Catherine stepped out. She quickly came back inside and tugged on Andrea's sleeve. Fear permeated her voice. "That man across the street. Is that the man Victoria saw?"

Ryan's heart pounded as he reached for the door to close it. His hand was on his gun. "Look out the window, Andrea, but don't stand in front of it."

Andrea took the few steps to the window and pulled back the curtain. "Yes, that's him. He must have asked around to find out Victoria was staying here."

"He saw me when I stepped out on the porch," said Catherine. "He'll think I'm Victoria."

"He's coming this way," said Andrea.

Ryan locked the front door. "We need to get out of here. Do you have a back door, and is there a neighbor's house you can go to?"

"This way." Andrea had already turned around.

They headed back down the hallway. The man was pounding on the door and it sounded like he was slamming against it.

They came to the back door. Ryan looked at Andrea. "When you get to your friend's house, call the police and say a man tried to break into your house. Have the police get in touch with me when they take him into custody."

Andrea opened the back door. "My friend's house is just across the alley."

"We're headed back to the car to try to get out of here," said Ryan. He couldn't put Andrea or her neighbor in any more danger. The pounding on the door had stopped.

He grabbed Catherine's hand as they both ran outside

toward the street. Catherine commanded the dogs to follow her. They got to the side of Andrea's house. Though it was growing dark, he could see the man was pacing the porch and staring in the windows as they made a run for the car.

Catherine opened the back door so the dogs could jump in.

The curly-haired man looked in their direction just as Catherine was getting into the passenger seat.

By the time the man bolted across the street to his dark blue SUV, they had pulled out on the street and were gaining speed.

"Let's see if we can shake this guy," said Ryan. He wanted to look for an opportunity to take the man into custody but that meant risking Catherine's safety. He hadn't seen any sign of the police yet. Assuming Andrea had phoned right away, they hadn't gotten there fast enough.

It took only minutes to get to the edge of town. Once there were no street lamps or light from houses, it grew even darker. Ryan focused on the road ahead as the yellow lines clipped by.

The other car gained on them. His heart pounded. He pressed the accelerator.

Catherine gripped the armrest. "He's too fast. We need to find a hiding place."

Adrenaline flooded his body as he looked side to side hoping to see an escape route. "You're the expert on this area."

He glanced over at her. Catherine's face had drained of color.

The other car was so close its headlights filled their vehicle.

"About a mile ahead." Her voice trembled as she spoke. "There's a right turn right after a field with round hay bales. You'll have to turn off your headlights so he can't see where we go." That meant he'd be driving blind.

The car drew within a few feet of them then tapped his back bumper.

Catherine gasped as she reached out for the dashboard.

Knowing he was risking an accident, Ryan pressed the accelerator to the floor.

At first, the other car matched his speed.

He came into a curve barely slowing as he gripped the wheel and prayed they'd stay on the road.

The move worked.

He'd put a little distance between them and the other car. He could just make out the field with the hay bales in the dim evening light. His headlights were still on.

"You see where the hay bales end," said Catherine. "The road is right there on the other side."

"I hope this works." He killed his headlights and made a guess at where the turnoff was. The jarring and bumping told him he hadn't found the road exactly. He rolled forward at a much slower pace until the terrain evened out.

There were no headlights behind them.

"Do you suppose we ditched him?"

"Keep going just to make sure," she said. "There's a cow shed up ahead and a wide spot in the road to turn around about hundred feet ahead. This road dead-ends on private property, so the only way out is to go back the way we came."

Not good. That meant they risked encountering the guy again.

He inched forward. When he heard grass brushing against the sides of the car, he knew he wasn't on the road. The shed was more shadow than substance, but he was able to get turned around.

They sat in the dark, both of them staring through the windshield for several minutes looking for headlights coming toward them.

"I think it worked. Don't want to take any chances, though. I'll drive blind to where this dirt road intersects with the highway. He might be waiting there for us."

He leaned forward to see better through the windshield, wishing that clouds hadn't covered the moon. Once he got to where he could pull out onto the highway, he stopped and let the car idle while he tried to see if there was another car parked anywhere. Several cars sped by on the paved road.

"I don't think he's around here." Her voice held a note of uncertainty.

Ryan wasn't sure what to do next. "We can't go back to town. That guy in the tan sedan is probably thinking we'll show up there."

"The man we just got rid of might go back there too." Her voice dropped half an octave. "Why are two men chasing me now?"

"Not sure exactly. Victoria recognized the man with the curly hair. He didn't look like anyone I've ever encountered in my undercover work. There's more than just one player in this smuggling operation and the guy might be hired muscle."

Catherine remained silent for a moment as if absorbing what he had said. They sat in the dark with the car idling. "What do we do now?"

He shifted. "Drive to the next town I guess, away from where we think those two men might be waiting. Hope we're not followed. I know Victoria said no police, but this is too big for me, I need to bring in some agents from the closest field office to help capture those men and see if we can set up a safe place for you."

His talk of putting Catherine in a safe house was met with silence.

It took him a moment to turn the headlights back on.

He still didn't see any sign of another vehicle tucked back in the shadows on the side of the road. He drove toward the paved road.

Catherine cleared her throat. "Do you think Victoria is still close?"

"I don't know what she is thinking or planning. She's afraid enough of that guy to run and leave behind her things. Maybe she'll leave the area."

He turned onto the road feeling a rising sense of frustration. With Victoria having vanished, the investigation was stalled out. The only lead now was the two men who were after her. He pulled his phone from his pocket. "We know what the guy looks like and what he drives. I need to get in touch with some local agents. With some help, maybe we can take the man with the curly hair in and question him. I assume he'll stick around and keep looking for you." The nearest field office was miles away in Bozeman since this area was nothing but small towns. It would take at least an hour for any agents to show up.

He drove a short distance while still looking to see if they were followed. He pulled over on the shoulder. "I have to make a call." To make sure they were not going to be followed, he wanted a chance to watch the road some more anyway.

He called and apprised the agent who answered the phone of the situation. He identified himself as Agent Evan Martin.

After Ryan summarized the situation, Agent Martin responded. "You're saying the guy knocked on the door and then followed you, but he wasn't violent toward you in any way?"

"No, he was, it sounded like he was trying to break in, and he did tap my car bumper before we shook him. According to Victoria Stevenson's friend, Victoria saw him as enough of a threat that she left town without stopping to pick up her possessions, some of which are evidence that I need to turn over to you."

"All our agents are engaged in a drug investigation at the moment, but we will try to get someone over to your area as fast as we can."

The guy didn't seem to think it was as urgent as Ryan did. "Can you at least let highway patrol in this area know in case they see either the car or the man I gave you a description of? The one we can't identify drives a tan sedan and the other is in a dark blue SUV."

"Yes, we can do that. Do you plan on staying in the area?"

"We need to get away from Lewisville." Staying here was too dangerous for Catherine. Victoria could be miles from here by now. "Actually, I need to talk to you about setting up a safe house for the woman who is being mistaken for Victoria Stevenson."

Catherine shifted in her seat at the mention of a safe house. As if picking up on her irritation, the dogs whined from the back seat.

"That too will take some time," said the agent on the phone. "We'll get to it as fast as we can."

Ryan gritted his teeth. "I'll be back in touch soon."

"I'll call you. I understand your need for help," said the other agent. "We've been in the middle of a drug-related case that has taken all our personnel. Maybe I can pull some agents from there."

"Or maybe I can get some support from local law enforcement." A note of irritation entered his voice. His preference would be to work with other agents, but he didn't like dealing with this alone. It put Catherine in that much more danger.

"I get what you're saying. I will put maximum effort into getting backup to you as quick as possible," said Agent Martin.

"Thank you."

He turned off the phone. While he was glad Agent Martin finally seemed to understand his situation, he felt no less frustrated. He pulled back onto the road. They passed a billboard that advertised a roadside café five miles away.

He hadn't eaten since breakfast before he'd rented the ATV. Would it be safe to stop? Only if he was sure they weren't followed.

"I'm hungry too," said Catherine, as if she had read his mind. "The dogs need to eat as well."

Dealing with their hunger was the least of their problems. Maybe by the time they were done eating, an FBI agent would be in touch and he could at least take steps to get Catherine some more protection.

Still nervous, he continued to check the rearview mirror and watch the road behind him.

Catherine picked up on Ryan's tension. He had fallen silent as he drove with only their headlights providing illumination on the dark lonely highway. Even though one car zoomed past going in the opposite direction and none came up behind them, she felt on edge. The day had almost been too much and her stomach was growling.

By the time they stopped at the roadside café, they'd be miles from where they'd last encountered the man with the brown curly hair.

"So who do you think those men are exactly?"

"Like I said, there is a turf war going on for control of the illegal diamond trade. I didn't recognize the one with the curly hair, but Victoria did. The man we encountered in the wilderness seemed most interested in finding the diamonds."

She laced her fingers together trying to quell some of the rising fear she felt when she thought about everything that had happened. "And the curly-haired man seemed to want to come after us, maybe to kill us?"

Ryan kept his eyes on the road. "I saw that he had a gun, so yes, maybe. I hope he doesn't go back to Andrea's house and that she let the police know the situation."

"I'm sure she will," she said.

"Once I get some support from other agents, we can keep eyes on Andrea's house to see if the curly-haired man returns. Then we might be able to catch him. Maybe the local cops will be able to take him into custody even sooner assuming Andrea called them."

"I don't want to go to a safe house. I've never been very good at staying inside."

"I get that, but they think you're Victoria. I'll work with the other agents to try to track down those two men. I can't do that with you out in the open. Those two men are the only lead I have right now. But I don't want to drag you into that kind of danger."

She was having a hard time accepting that being confined in a safe house was her only option.

A billboard for the roadside café came up saying it was a mile up the road. Ryan checked the rearview mirror one more time. There had been only one car behind them, and it had passed them.

"I know lots of places to hide. I've had some practice." From the time she was a small child, she had preferred the outdoors and sleeping beneath an open sky. The thought of being stuck in a house with curtains drawn made it hard to get a breath. Plus, she didn't like being reliant on Ryan.

"Catherine, don't argue with me. I feel a responsibility for having caused this trouble in your life," said Ryan.

"You make it worse by wanting to put me in a prison." It wasn't like she didn't have experience with this. She'd hidden from her ex-husband for over a year, but it had come with the freedom of being outdoors. "I feel safer out in the wilderness anyway."

His jaw tightened, though he didn't say anything.

The café came into view. Several streetlamps illuminated it. Bright lights shone from within. Ryan pulled into the paved lot where several other cars were parked. None of the cars looked familiar. A stand of trees and flat land surrounded the area. She was fairly sure the lights off in the distance must be farms or houses.

The only thing she was certain of right now was that she was starving. "Let me get some food for the dogs." Once he parked, she got out of the car and opened the trunk where she'd put the food and her other things.

Ryan watched the road while she got two bowls and poured food in each.

"Can they just eat in the car?" Ryan stepped toward her. "I don't think we should stay here long."

"Sure, I can do it that way." She opened the back door and placed the bowls on the back seat, petting each dog's head as they dug into the food. "You both were starving. I'm so sorry."

"Hopefully they will have some food we can grab quickly." He remained close to her as they stepped toward the entrance.

"From what I remember, I don't think they do take-out."

"You've been here before?"

"Yes." She pushed open the door. It had been years since she stopped at this café. When she was a teenager, she and her dad had often stopped here after they'd dropped off a load of grain at a nearby town. Her father always bought her a strawberry milkshake for helping with the farm labor, though it had never felt like work to her. She had fond memories of being outside helping her dad or working with the dogs.

They stepped inside.

A waitress wiping down a table looked up at them. "Find a seat anywhere."

Ryan glanced around. "You don't have a take-out menu?"

"Food will be just as fast if you sit down and relax," said the waitress.

Catherine noticed Ryan chose the seat in the booth that gave him a view of the door. He still hadn't totally let his guard down. Or maybe it was just habit as an agent to position himself where he had a panoramic view of the room.

The waitress set two menus on their table. "Be back in just a moment."

Ryan flipped open the menu. "What's good to eat here?"

"It's been years since I was in this place. The strawberry milkshake was always yummy. I think the burger or chicken basket is a pretty safe bet, and it won't take long for them to bring it out."

"Strawberry, you say. Sounds delicious but it might take a while to eat." He studied the back of the menu. "Guess the mushroom burger looks alright." He glanced toward the door when a man entered the café.

She followed the direction of Ryan's gaze to see a man with brown hair wearing a baseball cap and clothes stained from a day's work, probably doing something mechanical judging from the grease stains. Ryan seemed very tuned in to the movement of everyone in the room.

"There is no way he could find us here unless he followed us, right?" It sounded more like she was trying to convince herself as much as get assurances from Ryan.

"I know how jittery you must feel." Ryan's voice was filled with compassion. "Getting chased down for a day kind of makes a person stay on high alert."

The waitress returned and set down two glasses of water. "What can I get you?"

"I'll have the chicken basket and an orange soda," she said.

"Mushroom burger for me. Water is fine to drink."

The waitress gathered the menus and turned to leave.

Ryan sat his phone on the table and kept checking it. "If the agent doesn't get back to me soon, I'll see if the local police or sheriff can help. Only the FBI can help us with the safehouse though."

She took in a sharp breath when she thought about staying in a safe house. "I get to have a say in what happens in my life." She twirled her straw in the glass of water. "I can't stay inside for days on end. I feel the safest out in open country."

"Maybe we can find a place with a fenced yard, but even that has some risk," he said.

She took a sip of her water. Not wanting the disagreement to escalate, she wasn't sure what to say. She knew the level of danger she had encountered so far, but such confinement was just a hard reality to accept. "I've been taking care of myself for a long time."

"Look, I've seen it before where witnesses think they can deal with things alone. It never works out," His voice intensified as he emphasized each word. "It could be that if we can catch these two men and we are sure the threat against you is neutralized, you would be free to go back to work and your old life. I just can't take any chances right now."

She was drawn to the warmth she saw in his blue eyes. His clear desire to protect her melted some of the distrust she felt.

The waitress brought their meals, and they ate in silence. When they were almost finished, a man stepped inside. He glanced around the room. Catherine's heart beat a little faster. The man was a friend of Dave's. He made eye contact with her and then ambled over to the counter. Now for sure, word would get back to Dave. The man spoke to the waitress, who put a coffee cup in front of him. He took out his phone and started pressing buttons.

"Everything okay?"

She took her last two bites of food. "Can we go right now?"

He placed his unfinished burger down and stood up. He reached for the jacket he placed on the seat while he looked around the room. "What's going on?"

"The man that just came in and sat at the counter knows my ex-husband."

"Let's get out of here then. Where do you want to go?"

"As far away from here as possible." The fear that she would run into Dave was more visceral than any thought of an encounter with the other two men. Her instinct always was to get away from her ex-husband.

Ryan picked up his phone.

Now the idea of a safe house seemed like a good temporary measure.

They hurried out to the car where the dogs waited. After placing his phone on the console, Ryan pulled onto the road and drove into the night.

They'd only gone about five miles when his phone rang.

"Can you answer that? It's probably the agent I talked to."

She picked up the phone. "Hello?"

A woman's voice came through the line. "Catherine, is that you? I thought this was that FBI agent's number."

It took her a moment to realize it was Andrea on the other end.

"Yes, it's me. He's driving. I answered his phone. Is everything okay? Did you get in touch with the police? That man didn't come back to your house, did he?"

"I'm fine. I told the police. They've been patrolling the neighborhood, and I'm staying at my neighbors," said Andrea.

She breathed a sigh of relief to hear that Andrea was safe. "Oh, so what are you calling about?"

"You're who I wanted to talk to anyway. I didn't have your number."

"I'll text it to you." Catherine couldn't imagine the reason for the phone call. "Did you find something else important in Victoria's belongings?"

"No." Andrea took in an audible breath. "Victoria called me to find out if the man with the curly brown hair was still around. I told her he hasn't been around since I called the police when he tried to break in. I told her about you coming to look for her."

Catherine gripped the phone a little tighter. "What did she say?"

"She wants you to meet her at the farm," said Andrea.

A mixture of fear and hope threaded through Catherine's muscles. Her sister was still close by. "At the farm. Where?"

"She says you will know where to find her. Do you know what she meant by that?"

Catherine had to think for a moment. Far from the house and the outbuildings on the other side of the ranch was a tree house their father had built for them. Up until the time Victoria left to live with their mom, the tree house had been their special place. That had to be what she was talking about.

Though her cell phone was not viable when she was in the deep wilderness, Victoria had Catherine's number. It occurred to her why her sister was being so cryptic and circuitous with each message she got to Catherine. She probably feared her phone was bugged or her mail would be intercepted. "Did she say anything else?"

"When I told her that you were with an FBI agent named Ryan, she got upset. She said that you needed to come alone."

Once again, Catherine felt doubt about Ryan. He had seemed forthright with her. What did Victoria know that she didn't?

When she looked at Ryan, he glanced in her direction and then gazed back at the road.

"When am I supposed to meet her?"

"She said to meet her there in an hour. She instructed me to call her back and let her know if you can. She's calling from one of those throwaway phones. She said she would only answer if it was my number. Then she's getting rid of the phone."

Catherine pressed her lips together. She had no choice here. Victoria needed her help. Her sister was in trouble. "Tell her I'll be there."

"I'll do that," said Andrea.

"Thank you, I'll text you from my phone, so you'll have my number. You can call me directly if the plan changes."

Catherine hung up then sent a text to Andrea from her phone.

"I take it that wasn't the agent," said Ryan.

"My sister called Andrea. She knows I came to Lewisville to find her. She wants to meet me on the farm. I have to go alone."

"That's not a good idea," said Ryan.

"Whatever she's done, my sister isn't going to hurt me." Her voice took on a darker tone. "For some reason, she doesn't trust you."

"I never gave her any reason to doubt me. I don't know what's going on with her." Hurt permeated his words.

"All I know is my sister seems to think I am the only one she can trust. I need to go to her."

Ryan's jaw grew tight as he shook his head and let out a heavy breath. "I need to make contact with your sister. That's what I came to Montana to do."

"You mean you need to take her into custody," said Catherine.

"Look, if she did take those diamonds, there is a level of leniency because she was an informant. I need to find out the whole story from her."

"Please, I don't want to scare her away. Let me just go to her and find out what she knows and what she's done. She's afraid and has good reason to be because of that man she saw in town," Catherine said.

"Maybe you can convince her that I have her best interest at heart," said Ryan.

Catherine wasn't sure what to think about Ryan. She'd just started to trust him and then Victoria's admonition that she come alone spun her head around. "I'm the one she wants to tell her side of the story to. I'm the one she trusts."

"This goes against all kinds of protocol. We should have a team watching the place where you plan to meet."

"That would take time and for sure that would scare her away. Whatever my sister has done, she is still my sister and I love her. I'm not in danger. She's not violent. She wouldn't hurt me that way." The pain her sister had caused had all been emotional, but it had left wounds.

"I'll have to take your word for that. You said your relationship was strained."

"I think I know my sister way better than you do." Catherine stared up at the night sky through the windshield. Frustration made her curl her hand into a fist.

"I have a duty as an agent." Ryan emphasized each word as he spoke.

"Maybe I can convince her to turn herself in. You can't. She doesn't trust you for whatever reason." Catherine wrestled with her own doubt. Her sister wouldn't hurt her physically. She was confident about that much. But in many ways, she didn't know Victoria anymore. Maybe she had taken those diamonds.

Ryan drove for several minutes without saying anything. "I'll get turned around as soon as I can find a spot. Andrea must have your sister's phone number. Can you get it from her? Why don't we try to communicate with her directly?"

"Andrea said Victoria is using burner phones and discarding them," she said. "I doubt she would answer."

"She really doesn't want to be found or traced."

The road signs indicated they were getting closer to a larger town. Traffic was heavier here. Cars passed them and others lingered behind.

She felt tightening in her chest. She had to go to her sister and help her. She was the only one who could, but it meant returning to the area where they might encounter the men who thought she was Victoria.

EIGHT

Ryan watched the road for a wide shoulder so he could turn around and head back to the farm. "When are you supposed to meet her?"

"In an hour," said Catherine. "It's at a remote part of the farm."

"How big is your farm?"

"Over three hundred acres," she said.

It didn't sit well with Ryan that Catherine had doubts about him. He had done nothing to destroy trust between himself and Victoria. Yet, for some reason she didn't want to come to him for help, and Catherine believed her estranged sister over anything he could say to her. What little trust had been built between them seemed easily broken.

"What am I supposed to do while you go meet your sister?"

"Wait for me far enough away so she doesn't see you," she said. "I'll tell her that the FBI can provide protection for her. Maybe she would be willing to work with another agent."

Maybe it would come to that, but this was his case.

He slowed as the road widened with a passing lane up ahead, still searching for a place to turn around. There were a few cars behind him, as well as several going in the opposite direction.

He saw a wide shoulder up ahead and slowed even more.

Once he got turned around, he sped up. "Is there any quick way to get back to your farm?"

"No, I'll let you know when we are getting close to the turnoff and then I'll give you directions to where we need to go."

A car passed them while another vehicle remained behind them for miles. When he slowed down, the car did as well. Not a good sign. It was too dark to clearly see the make and model of the vehicle. The headlights were high up, so it was probably a truck. Neither of the men who had come after them before drove a truck.

A tense silence permeated the interior of the car.

Catherine shifted in her seat. "Look, all I want to do is help my sister."

"You don't think I want that too?" He sounded more defensive than he had intended. "Have I done or said anything to indicate I would harm you or your sister?"

"No," she said softly.

"My job is to bring her in," said Ryan.

"And if you scare her away, that won't happen. Let me talk to her alone."

What he really wanted was for Catherine to say that she trusted and believed in him. He always tried to do the right thing, the lawful thing. Couldn't she see that? His confidence as an agent had been shaken by past betrayals, and now she was eroding it even more.

He drove through the darkness without talking anymore.

Catherine spoke up. "The turnoff is in about three miles. You'll have to slow way down to see it. There are no lights out here."

The truck was still behind them, so he sped up to put some distance between them before he made the turn onto the dirt road that led to the farm. After stopping, he killed the lights. No sign of the truck coming toward them. He pressed the gas and kept going.

She pulled her phone from her satchel. "I'll call Celeste and Ralph and let them know not to be alarmed if they see our headlights. We won't be going close to the house, but I don't want them to worry that a stranger is on the farm."

She made the call but it went unanswered so she left a message. "They must already be asleep."

"Where is it I'm taking you?"

"There's a little spur road up ahead here that veers off away from the farmhouse and outbuildings. I'll let you know when we're getting close."

She told him where to turn. The road had a washboard quality, probably from years of harsh weather and no maintenance.

"Stop here," she said. "I'll walk the rest of the way."

He didn't see anything but a line of tall trees planted as a windbreak in the distance. The time to try to convince her he should go with her had passed. She was right. If Victoria didn't trust him, his showing up would scare her away, maybe for good. Still the plan did not sit well with him. "How far do you have to walk?"

"She will meet me at a tree house that my father built. The walk will take me less than ten minutes." She pushed open the door. "I'm taking the dogs with me. I'm sure Victoria would like to see Liz."

"Can you at least text or call me that you made contact with her?"

"I can only do that with her permission after we talk. So much depends on what she has to tell me," said Catherine. "I will try to convince her to come out of hiding but no promises."

Once she unloaded the dogs, he left the headlights on so she could see to pull her phone out of her purse and turn on the flashlight. He watched as she became nothing more than shadow and a bobbing light headed toward the trees.

His phone rang. "Yes," he said.

"This is Agent Martin from the Bozeman field office. Just wanted to let you know we were able to pull two agents off our operation, and they are in the Lewisville area now looking for the cars and the man you described. I've texted you their numbers so you can have direct contact with them, Agent Bronson and Agent Fields."

"That's good news. Let me know if you take either man in. I need to be there for the questioning."

"Will do. Also, we're working on finding a safe place for your witness."

"Thank you, Agent Martin. Be in touch."

Once he disconnected from the call, silence settled into the car. He couldn't see Catherine or the dogs anymore.

He switched off the headlights and hunkered down behind the wheel. If Victoria drove past, she wouldn't see him.

He didn't think either of the two men were close by.

And yet, an uneasy feeling settled in his chest.

Catherine chose her steps carefully over the bumpy ground. It had been years since she'd been out here to the tree house. Though she and her sister had spent many happy hours in it when they were young, once Victoria left with their mom as a teen, coming to this place had just seemed lonely.

The tree house had been built in two parts. The lower half on the ground was a single room with walls, windows and a door. A ladder on the flat roof led up to where there was a platform with a railing resting on two sturdy branches. She wouldn't trust the ladder after all these years.

As she stood outside the tree house, she aimed the flashlight on her phone all around the area, not seeing a car or any sign of Victoria. She moved closer to the line of trees and shone her light past. There was a road on the other side of the trees that Victoria might use to access the tree house. She saw nothing but the flat landscape.

Ducking her head, Catherine stepped into the lower half of the structure. Though the wood was weathered by time, her father had built the house to last. There was still evidence that she and Victoria had played here as children and been happy, a broken teacup, a plastic chair, a torn book weathered by time. All the artifacts of a more innocent time.

She shone her light through the window that faced the opposite direction from where she had come. Nothing but darkness. How long should she wait? It had taken a little less than an hour to get here. What if Victoria got cold feet?

She found an old plastic and metal chair in the corner of the room. After testing it for stability, she sat down. The dogs settled at her feet.

The wind blew through the glassless windows as tree branches rustled and creaked above her.

She heard the faint hum of a car engine but did not see any lights anywhere. Her first thought was that Ryan had broken his word and was coming toward her with no headlights, but when she stared out the window that faced where she'd come from, she didn't see anything. Not even any movement. She could just make out the outline of her car in the distance.

Growing restless, the dogs circled around her, and she moved to the other side of the playhouse. The engine noise had stopped. Her heart beat a little faster. Victoria was out there and had accessed the tree house from the other side of the farm.

A woman screamed in the dark. A car started up. Catherine burst through the door of the playhouse. "Victoria! Don't go. I'm here."

She ran into a solid mass of flesh. A strong hand gripped her upper arm.

"Sorry, I scared your sister away. I thought she was you." It was her ex-husband, Dave. His voice was like stabs to her body. Her knees buckled as her heart pounded.

Fear struck her to the marrow of her bones. Her wrist hurt as he squeezed her hand tighter. "How did you find me here?"

"I saw you were going to the farm," Dave said.

"You followed us in your truck?" She was shaking from fear.

"I wasn't far from the roadside café when my friend said he'd seen you," he said. "On the flat land of this farm, you can see headlights for miles. I saw where you were going and circled around."

"Please, I have someone with me, helping me. He's waiting in the car."

"Who? The guy my friend saw you with at the café. I'm sure he's long gone." His words dripped with sarcasm. "I know you, Catherine, so convinced you can do everything by yourself."

The dogs had begun to yip in protest as they circled around her and Dave. When Betty put her paws on Dave's leg, he kicked her.

"Don't you dare!"

Not wanting the dogs to be hurt anymore, she gave the command for them to back off and sit. They retreated toward the tree house.

"You're coming with me." He dragged her across the grass. "No wife of mine just up and leaves me."

She screamed Ryan's name. Dave placed a hand over her mouth and the other around her waist, pressing her against his chest and lifting her feet off the ground. She tried to twist free but his grip on her was iron tight.

As he carried her, she could see his truck more clearly.

He let go of her and pulled a gun from a holster attached to his belt. "You're going to drive and you're not going to try anything. Got it?"

She nodded. He opened the cab of the truck and pushed on her back. She climbed in. He pointed the gun at her through the windshield as he hurried around to the passenger side and got in.

Still keeping the gun close to her head, he pulled keys from his shirt pocket.

She didn't need to ask him what his intent was. He hated her for divorcing him and would make good on his promise to kill her.

He probably just wanted to go somewhere her body wouldn't be found, so he would never be caught.

Her hand was shaking as she put the key in the ignition. She reached to turn on the headlights as an idea struck her. She turned them on and off in an SOS pattern.

"Stop that. Just turn them on and leave them on."

The trees probably mostly obscured the lights anyway, but maybe Ryan had seen.

"I'm sorry. My hands are shaking. I'm just very nervous." Dave's words about her always thinking she had to do everything by herself whirled through her mind.

Ryan had wanted to protect her, and she had pushed him away. Why? Out of habit, believing that she could only depend on herself? There might have been a way for him to be close without alarming Victoria, but she hadn't even considered it. Was it that her trust in men had been so broken by being with Dave that she couldn't receive help when it was offered to her?

Her stubborn independence would be her downfall. She saw that now.

"Get turned around. We'll use the back road to get off the farm."

She felt hope fading. That route meant they wouldn't go anywhere near where Ryan was parked waiting for her.

She knew her ex-husband well enough that trying to talk him out of anything would be pointless. Their whole marriage he was convinced that everything that was wrong was her fault.

The truck lumbered over the grass until she saw the rutted dirt road up ahead.

"You can go faster now, you know," he said.

She didn't dare speed up, knowing that she was driving to her death.

NINE

As Ryan drove closer to the line of trees designed to be a wind break, a two-tiered tree house came into view. That had to be where Catherine was meeting Victoria. It did not sit well with him to stay behind, and when enough time had passed that Catherine should have texted him, he knew something wasn't right.

He'd thought he'd seen lights flash through the thick of the trees, but he wasn't sure.

He got out and walked toward the tree house. The dogs bounded out to meet him. "Hey there. Where's your owner?" He hurried the remaining distance to the tree house, shining the flashlight from his phone on the empty interior.

The dogs continued to circle him in a nervous way. Feeling a rising tension, he called out Catherine's name twice. He heard only the sound of the wind through the tall cottonwoods.

His hand curled into a fist, and he shook his head. Catherine wouldn't leave the dogs behind unless she had no choice.

His stomach twisted tight as the silence enveloped him. Something was wrong. He stepped out of the tree house.

He saw red taillights in the distance through the trees. Was it possible Victoria had intended to hurt her sister?

Taken her as a hostage? Or maybe she just needed Catherine to come with her for some reason.

"Come on, let's get loaded up." He ran back to the car with the dogs right beside him. He'd have to drive the length of the windbreak to get on the other side of it. The flat land on this part of the farm meant he could see the taillights from a long way off.

He pressed the gas and drove until the trees ended. Because of the bumpy ground, he was only able to speed up a little bit. Glancing off to the side through the trees, he kept track of the red taillights as they grew smaller while he searched the landscape for a road.

His tires rolled much easier and faster once he found the dirt surface that qualified as a road. He sped up.

What was going on here?

He feared that if Catherine was safe, she would have texted him like she'd promised. Feeling a sense of urgency, he drove even faster.

The problem with the flat open country was that the driver would see him too and know she was being followed if he got too close. The road was flat and straight. Still going as fast as he dared, he turned off his headlights.

The other vehicle stopped when it came to a crossroads at what must be the edge of the farm. Ryan was able to get close enough to see that the vehicle was a truck. It pulled out onto a paved road. Ryan hung back. There were no other cars visible at this late hour. He kept his eyes on the taillights as he turned onto the paved road and switched his own headlights back on. He could follow for a few miles before the driver of the truck got suspicious.

The truck sped up.

Ryan did not but made sure he didn't lose sight of the

truck. It had only gone a few miles when the left-hand signal started to blink.

Was the driver aware she was being followed and trying to shake him?

He saw up ahead where the truck had turned onto a dirt road. He took that road as well, which led him to rolling hills. He'd lost visual on the truck, but it had to be on this road. He'd passed no other places to turn off.

He came up to the rise of a hill. Down below, the truck had pulled over. He watched as a man, not a woman, got out of the passenger side and pulled a woman from the driver's seat.

His breath hitched when he realized the woman was Catherine.

He rolled down the hill and pulled over about twenty yards from the truck. The man had hauled Catherine to the front side of the truck. If he stayed there, he wouldn't see Ryan approaching. The truck would obstruct his view. Ryan flung open the door reaching for his gun as he stalked toward the truck.

He walked faster when he heard Catherine scream in protest.

Using the truck to shield himself, he peered above the rim of the truck bed. The man had a gun and was pushing Catherine toward a stand of trees.

If he announced himself and held up his gun, he'd be risking Catherine's life.

Between the truck and the trees there was no place to take cover. He stayed low to the ground and moved as stealthily as he could.

The man's build could be that of the helmeted rider whose face he had never seen. That man had been keenly interested in finding the diamonds. Would he hold a gun to Catherine's head believing she was Victoria to get her to confess where the gems were?

His foot slid on some rocks. The noise seemed to augment in the nighttime silence. The other man turned, grabbing Catherine by the collar before he did. Ryan dropped to the ground praying the darkness would conceal him.

The man stared for a long moment.

Ryan's pulse pounded in his ears. He dared not even take a breath. A bit of moonlight allowed Ryan to see the glint of the man's gun as he swung it in a slow arc.

The man jerked Catherine by the collar, swinging her around and then pushing the gun into her back.

Once Catherine and the man disappeared into the trees, Ryan sprinted to get to her before it was too late. The closer he got, the slower he moved.

It grew darker once the trees enveloped him.

He picked up on the sound of footsteps and several grunts. Then a cry of protest from Catherine that seemed to get cut off.

He thought he heard her say, "Please, Dave, no."

Was this man Catherine's ex-husband?

He moved with a light footstep toward the sounds, fearing that the next noise would be a gunshot.

The cold metal of the gun barrel dug into her back as Dave pushed Catherine deeper into the trees. Her mind raced at a hundred miles an hour.

"Please, Dave, don't do this. I know you think you won't get caught—"

"Shut up."

The truth is he probably wouldn't get charged even if her body was found in this remote place. The local police department wouldn't point the finger at him.

If she could distract him and pull the gun out of his hand, maybe she could get back to the truck before he caught her. He had put on some pounds, and she was in good shape from the hiking and climbing her job required.

She pivoted so she was sideways to him. The gun was in his right hand.

If she tried to get it away and failed, he'd shoot her on the spot. She knew him well enough to know that rage made most of his decisions for him.

"Turn around and keep going. We need to get deeper into the forest, so they don't ever find you."

She prayed silently to herself.

She heard a thud and then the pressure of the gun was no longer on her back.

Her heart flooded with gratitude when she saw Ryan jumping on top of Dave and wrestling him to the ground. He had figured out that something was not right and had come after her.

Dave's gun lay on the ground. Ryan scrambled to his feet and aimed his gun at Dave's back where he still lay on his stomach. "Don't you try anything. I'm Agent McCloud and I'm taking you into custody. Now stand up nice and slow."

"Ryan, this is my ex-husband, Dave Reed."

He didn't answer right away. His gaze stayed on Dave and then he glanced at Catherine. "So I gathered."

Once he was on his feet and turned around, Dave lunged at Ryan. The gun went off. Both men were still standing. Dave punched Ryan in the jaw. The gun fell from his hand.

Ryan dove for the gun, retrieving it, but Dave jumped on his back. The two men wrestled.

Catherine reached down to get Dave's gun where it had fallen. She lifted the gun to aim it. In the dark, it was hard to see any separation between the two men.

"Get off of him right now, or I'll shoot."

Dave glanced in her direction and it was enough for her to know where to aim.

The momentary inattention gave Ryan the chance to get on his feet.

Dave reached toward Ryan's gun where it had fallen. Ryan placed his boot on Dave's hand, causing the man to cry out in pain. Ryan retrieved the gun himself. Aiming the gun at Dave who was still on the ground, he took a step back. "Like I said, stand up nice and slow with your hands in the air."

Grunting, Dave pushed himself to his feet.

"Oh, come on now, Catherine. I'm sorry about this." Dave spoke in a tone of voice she recognized, fake contrition. How many times had she fallen for that when they were married? How many times had she wanted to believe he was sincere because she wanted the marriage to work?

Did he really think that would have an effect on her now that she saw him so clearly?

Dave looked at Ryan. "Look, I see you're trying to help but you don't know this woman. She likes to make up stories." His voice had taken on a soft quality.

Catherine clenched her teeth. Now Dave was trying to manipulate Ryan.

Ryan held his gun steady. "Catherine, I'm a witness here that this man kidnapped you and attempted to murder you. I'll see to it that charges are brought against him."

"You can't turn him over to the local police."

"I get that. I know what to do," said Ryan. He turned his attention to Dave. "Now let's take it real slow and head back to the vehicles. Keep your hands up where I can see them."

For the first time since she'd seen going into hiding as her only option, Catherine felt hopeful that this time Dave would go to jail, thanks to Ryan. It was a comfort to her to know he was on her side. Not since her father had died had she felt like she had that in her life.

They started the march back to the cars.

Dave turned his head sideways as Ryan and Catherine walked behind him, both still aiming the guns at him. "What about my truck?"

"You'll have to make arrangements for a friend to come get it," said Ryan.

Once back at the cars, Ryan addressed Catherine. "Open the back door of the car so he can sit in there. Let the dogs out for now."

Catherine obliged. "What's going to happen now?"

Dave sat in the car with his head down.

"I'll have my contacts at the closest field office make arrangements to have him put in a jail not in this county and make sure charges are filed." He pulled the phone out. "Let me make the call. We might have to drive him there, but I want to see if another agent is close by, so you don't have to be in the car with him. Keep the gun aimed at him just to be on the safe side."

Dave barely lifted his head when she stood by the window with the gun. She saw him for who he really was, a coward.

Ryan took a few steps away from the car to make his call. She caught only pieces of the conversation.

He turned to face her as he clicked a button on his phone. "There's an agent ten minutes away who can come for him. They did show up to comb the area to look for the vehicles and the man whose face we saw."

"That's good." She was glad not to have a long car ride with Dave. And she sure didn't want the dogs to have to endure being near him. Judging from Ryan's actions he'd probably realized how frightening that would have been for her. She appreciated his sensitivity to the situation. In fact, she found herself appreciating a lot of things about Ryan.

"And they have a safe house set up for you. The agent gave me the location."

She didn't object, but her back stiffened.

"What exactly happened back at the tree house? Did Victoria even show up?"

"Dave scared her away," she said.

He ran his hands through his hair. "You didn't get to talk to her at all?" He sounded frustrated.

"I heard a car start up and she drove away," said Catherine.

"I don't know what is going on with your sister. The other agents might locate her if she stays in the area," said Ryan.

"Maybe Victoria will try again. She might get in touch with Andrea to reach me."

"If she has those diamonds, she has the connections to slowly sell them off and enough money to leave the country."

"She wants to talk to me for some reason. She's tried twice."

"And she got scared off twice," said Ryan. "I know you don't like the idea, but you need some protection until we can catch those two men."

"You were right. I'm sorry I argued with you." Ryan taking Dave into custody had shifted her impression of him. She knew she could trust him at least as a law officer…and maybe in other ways too. "I hope they track down those men quickly. That's all I can say."

Dave's words about her always believing she had to do everything alone made her realize that thinking that way had almost gotten her killed.

They waited until the other agent, a tall blond woman named Agent Fields, showed up to take Dave into custody.

As he was led off toward the car, Dave gave her a backward glance, grinning in a way that his teeth showed. It sent a chill down her spine.

Ryan came up behind her and placed a supportive hand on her upper back. "The charges will stick this time. I'll see to that."

His touch calmed her. "I hope you're right. His family has money. They'll hire lawyers."

"I saw how he treated you. I'll do everything I can to make sure justice is served."

A weight lifted off her, and it was all because of Ryan. "Thank you. You don't know what it means to have someone on my side."

He gave her arm a reassuring squeeze. "Let's get you to that safe house."

She grabbed his arm. "No, I mean it. For the first time since I went into hiding, it feels like my life might get back to normal someday after all this is over."

His voice held a warmth she hadn't heard before. "Just trying to help out where I can."

Catherine didn't know why Victoria was afraid of Ryan; all she knew was that he'd proven himself to be someone who would risk his own life to protect her.

They got the dogs loaded up. While she settled into the passenger seat, he checked a map on his phone.

Except for light from the stars, the road was dark until they got back out to the paved road. Once the road beneath the tires was smooth, she could feel herself nodding off.

"I'm sleepy. You must be tired too," she said.

"Getting there."

Ryan's voice seemed to come from far away as she rested her head against the window and slept.

She was awakened when by a jarring bump that caused her to bite her tongue. A second later, the car lurched violently.

She turned her head as glaring headlights filled her vision.

Someone was trying to run them off the road.

TEN

The car seemed to have come out of nowhere. It was the dark blue SUV the curly-haired man drove. Fatigue had made Ryan drop his guard. Though he was more prepared for the second bump, it was much harder. He veered into the other lane, grateful there was no oncoming traffic.

Catherine gripped the handrest and let out a cry. The dogs yelped from the back seat.

The man was going so fast that his car went halfway off the road. The car tires rolled over the grass for twenty feet before he could get back on the pavement and turn into his own lane.

How had they even been found? The guy must have followed the agent, figuring she might lead him to them. The agent would have identified herself while in town asking questions. That had to be it.

The other car moved into the right lane and evened up with Catherine's car. The driver swung the wheel and bashed into the side of their car.

Ryan tried speeding up. The other driver kept pace with him and scraped the side of the car again. A screeching noise filled the air as metal rubbed against metal. Ryan gripped the wheel in an effort to keep the car on the road.

He hit the brakes and did a turn on the empty road as

the other car sped ahead. The maneuver put some distance between his car and the other driver while he got turned around, but they were headed in the opposite direction from the safe house.

Maybe it was for the best. They needed to shake this guy before they went there.

The other driver gained on them. The needle moved past eighty, but Ryan slowed when the road grew curvier. With only his headlights providing a degree of illumination, he strained to see the road ahead.

They were headed back to town.

Catherine's voice wavered as she spoke. "You could maybe cut through the farm and get turned back around. Lose him by making a sudden turn like we did last time."

"You have to tell me when the turnoff for the farm is coming up."

Headlights filled his rearview mirror.

Catherine leaned forward to peer through the windshield. "It's not far. Maybe another five minutes. Remember, you'll see the water tower."

It was hard to see anything in the dark. Everything looked different at night.

The other car was within twenty feet of them.

"There, now," Catherine said.

He made the turn, missing the road by a few feet and bumping along. The other car turned as well and crashed into their bumper, driving them farther into a ditch by the road.

The impact jarred his body.

The other driver backed up, engine still racing as though prepared to make another run at them.

Their car chugged forward making grinding noises. They were stuck in the ditch. "We have to get out of here." Adrenaline coursed through his body as his heart pounded.

Catherine had already opened the passenger side door, which faced away from where the other car stood revving its engine.

The driver of the other car got out, using the door as shield and taking aim with a gun.

Ryan pulled his gun as the first shot impacted the back window. Catherine had just let the dogs out of the far side of the car and took off running.

Ryan crawled across the front seat and slipped out of the passenger side. He lifted his head to get a visual on the other man, who still shielded himself behind the car door.

When he looked in the other direction, Ryan could just make out the white coloring on the dogs as they ran alongside Catherine. He sprinted toward them.

Another gunshot reverberated behind him. Ryan stumbled but kept running. Catherine seemed to have a plan of where to go. They were on the far side of the farm close to the tree house and line of trees planted as a windbreak, but not close to the farmhouse and outbuildings.

They passed tall cottonwoods and he could hear the rippling of a creek, though he could not see it.

She slowed so he could catch up.

When he looked over his shoulder, he saw a bobbing light headed toward them but in sort of a serpentine pattern. The guy didn't know exactly where they were.

The sound of water flowing over rocks grew louder. Catherine's boots made a splashing sound as she and the dogs crossed the creek. Ryan followed, feeling the water soak through his boots. His ankle still hurt a little.

The noise of them moving through the creek would have been enough for the pursuer to hone in on where they were. She kept running across an open field that had been plowed. He took big strides jumping over the furrows. There were no trees or brush close by to conceal them. The bobbing light edged closer to them.

He could see the tree windbreak, but it had to be at least a half mile away. Because this part of the farm was open and flat, there was no place to hide. Only the darkness provided them a degree of cover. The pursuer gained on them, closing the distance. He had a light to guide his footsteps while they ran in the dark.

They came to a field filled with round hay bales. Catherine and the dogs slipped behind one and Ryan edged in close to her, their shoulders pressed together. They were both gasping for breath.

He angled around the hay bale, not seeing the pursuer's light anywhere. She ran to the next hay bale and then another until they were almost to the edge of the field.

The pursuer might be slowed by having to check each hay bale, but they couldn't stay here for long without being found.

"How far away are we from the farmhouse?"

"A mile or more," she said. Her words came out between breaths. "It's too far and I don't want to put Celeste and Ralph in danger."

He still had his phone. Maybe that other agent close by could get to them before the curly-haired man did.

The zing of a bullet in the air told him there was no time to make a call. Catherine ran toward another hay bale. He followed.

Straw poked into his back as he pressed against the bale. Out of his peripheral vision, he saw flashes of light. The man with the curly hair was still searching the hay bales for them.

His heart pounded as they both fell silent. Footsteps seemed to surround them.

The pursuer's car was still operational even if theirs

wasn't. Maybe they could double back and use it to get away. More footsteps indicated the guy was too close.

If they tried to run now, they'd be spotted. The dogs pressed close to Catherine's legs. Both he and Catherine remained still, watching the light get closer to where they were hidden.

His heart pulsed in his ears as he considered their options; none of them good.

How were they going to escape?

Catherine squeezed her eyes shut hoping to be able to tell where the pursuer was from the sound of his footsteps. She couldn't see the light anymore. The noise of feet padding on soft earth and fallen straw seemed to echo. It was impossible to pinpoint where the pursuer was, other than he was close enough for her to hear his footsteps.

Her muscles tensed as she waited. She could no longer hear the footfall.

Maybe he wasn't as close as he sounded, or he could have turned off the flashlight. He could be standing very still too. It was hard to tell.

Ryan tugged on her sleeve. Staying low, he hurried toward a hay bale at the edge of the field and hid on the end of it. She followed him. He put his finger to his lips indicating they needed to be quiet and then he pointed beyond the field.

They were facing the creek and the cottonwoods where they'd just come from. He wanted to go back the way they'd come. To get the other guy's car?

She'd have to trust that he had a plan. She nodded.

He stepped out from the cover of the hay bales, choosing his steps carefully.

A gunshot shattered the nighttime quiet. Ryan did an

about-face and they ran back toward the hay bales. The guy was watching the edge of the field so they couldn't get back to the functioning car.

They both pressed against the first hay bale they came to. "Look, we have no choice. We need to go to the farm and get some help," Ryan whispered.

She didn't like putting Ralph and Celeste in danger, but they were out of options. Still trying to catch her breath, she nodded.

Ryan moved to the hay bale on the edge of the field that faced away from the windbreak. He burst forward going only a short distance before dropping to the ground. She followed, expecting more gunshots. Her stomach rested against the hard-packed dirt.

As she lay on the ground with the dogs beside her, silence surrounded her. She turned her head back toward the hay field where light traveled over the top rim of a hay bale in the middle of the field. The guy thought they were still hiding in the hay bales. This would give them a chance to put some distance between them and the man.

Ryan rose and kept running. She and the dogs caught up with him.

He slowed down. "Which way?"

She pointed toward an open flat area with no buildings in sight.

Her feet pounded the grassy earth. When she peered over her shoulder, the light was at the edge of the hay field.

They kept running until they reached a copse of trees. She leaned against a trunk gasping for air. The bobbing light was some distance from them but still moving.

Ryan touched her arm. "We have to keep going."

She jogged across the terrain as fast as she dared in the

darkness. The dogs seemed more surefooted than she was, so she followed the path they chose.

The light moved up and down around the trees they had just come through, which meant the pursuer thought they were hiding there.

They ran for at least ten minutes. She gasped for air but kept going.

The silhouettes of the outbuildings on the edge of the farm came into view. Her legs ached from the exertion of fleeing.

She could no longer see the bobbing light behind them. Was it possible he'd given up or gone searching for them elsewhere or maybe he'd gone back to get his car?

They kept going. She was grateful when the lamppost outside the farmhouse shone like a beacon. They were almost there.

They ran the remaining distance. Catherine stepped up on the porch. Only the light in the living room was on. She knocked on the door, knowing she would probably be getting Ralph and Celeste out of bed.

More lights came on inside. Ralph opened the door with a bleary-eyed Celeste standing behind him.

"Catherine, what's going on?"

Ryan stepped forward. "We're in a bit of a dilemma. If we could come inside so I can make a call."

Ralph hesitated.

Catherine spoke up. "Please, I'm sorry to do this. But we're in some danger and we need to get help."

Ralph glanced back at his wife who nodded. He opened the door wider. They stepped inside.

Catherine grabbed Ralph's arm. "A man may be after us. We'll get out of here as quickly as possible."

Celeste moved closer to her husband. "Does this have

something to do with Victoria coming back here? I told Ralph about her being in trouble and you looking for her."

"Yes," said Catherine. "But things have gotten very complicated."

Ralph moved to the window and peered out. "I don't see anything out there."

Ryan pulled out his phone. "If I could just make a call, there might be an agent close by who can come for us. We don't want to stay here longer than we have to."

Celeste moved to turn on a living room lamp. "Those poor dogs look ragged. I'm sure they could use some water."

While Ryan made his call, Catherine led the dogs into the kitchen where Celeste pulled two bowls from the cupboard and filled them with water. The dogs drank greedily.

This was taking a toll on them as well. "Celeste, can the dogs stay here with you? Just until I can get things resolved with Victoria." She hated the idea of being separated from them.

"Sure, honey. You know they would both love to have the run of the farm."

Ryan stood in the kitchen doorway. "It's all set. An agent should pick us up in twenty minutes."

She nodded. This probably meant she'd be taken to a safe house and Ryan would try to track down the two men who'd come after them, since Victoria had gone silent. How long would she have to stay there? She'd been in hiding from Dave, and now she would have to be in hiding again, only now it wouldn't be in her beloved wilderness.

She kneeled down to pet Betty and Liz when they were done drinking, running her fingers through their silky soft fur. "I'm leaving these two here. They have been through enough." Betty licked her face. Her throat went tight at the thought of leaving them.

Ryan leaned to pet Liz behind the ears. "Probably for the best. They'll be safe here."

Ryan drew his attention back to the living room. "I need to watch the house. If that guy is going to show up, it will more likely be in the next twenty minutes." He drew his gun and headed toward the door, probably to patrol the outside of the house.

When she peered into the living room, Ralph was already checking out each window.

They weren't in the clear yet.

ELEVEN

Ryan stepped outside. He walked to the end of the porch and studied the landscape in the direction he and Catherine had just come. He breathed a little deeper when after few minutes of watching, he saw no bobbing light.

He stepped off the porch and strode a little farther out, waiting for his eyes to adjust to the darkness once he was no longer close to the lamppost. Still nothing.

He turned back toward the house. Maybe it would be worth it to get law enforcement to stay close even after he and Catherine left. Chances were the guy would find another means of attack like going back to his car and waiting at the entrance to the farm. All the same, Ralph and Celeste deserved the assurance of some protection.

Stepping back toward the house, he saw that Ralph was still moving nervously from window to window. Ryan remained on the porch resting his forearms on the railing and watching for any sign of movement or light.

Catherine had grown up here. He heard the mixture of affection and angst in her voice anytime she talked about this farm. Maybe now that her violent ex-husband was most likely going to be out of the picture, she could return to the place she clearly loved. But that couldn't happen as long as those two men were out there and thought she was Victoria.

He found himself thinking about her more and more. Shortly, he'd be handing her over to the agent in the safe house. They'd known each other less than a day and yet he was drawn to her strong, independent nature. Every once in a while, a hint of vulnerability showed through that guarded nature, which was endearing. All the same, he knew in his heart that his life and his work were back in Seattle. Once this case was wrapped up, he'd be headed home. No need to contemplate there being anything between them. He couldn't help it if his thoughts kept returning to her.

Catherine and Victoria were dead ringers for each other in appearance but personality wise, they were two very different people.

When he stepped back into the house, Catherine sat on the couch holding a steaming mug. Liz lay on the floor on Catherine's feet and Betty had taken up a position on the couch, resting her muzzle on Catherine's thigh. The image of affection between the three touched him. It had to be hard to leave the dogs behind.

She gazed up at him, a soft smile gracing her face. "Celeste made some cocoa if you want some." She gestured toward the kitchen where Celeste was wiping down a counter.

Ralph had settled into an easy chair that provided him a view through the front windows.

"Thanks, but I should keep watch," said Ryan.

He returned to the window that looked out on the driveway, expecting to the see the headlights of the agent's car at any moment.

Liz padded across the wood floor and sat down beside him. He kneeled to pet her head and rub behind her ears. "I'm going to miss you too."

When he stood to check the window again, he saw headlights in the distance. His hand touched his gun. Would the curly-haired pursuer have had time to get back to his car and come around to the other farm entrance?

He couldn't take any chances.

Ralph sat up straighter in his chair. Catherine looked toward the window as well.

Ryan held up a hand. "I got this." He watched as the car drew closer. The man with the curly hair had driven a dark blue SUV. This car was a lighter color, probably tan or beige.

Ralph retreated to the kitchen to where his wife was. Catherine had risen to her feet.

"Is it the agent?" Tension threaded through her voice.

"I think so," he said. The car came to a full stop partially illuminated by the lamppost. Not the pursuer's car. Ryan turned to face Catherine. "Time to go."

She bent over and nuzzled her face close to Betty's. "I'll be back. I promise." She gave Liz a final pet as well.

Celeste stood in the doorway between the kitchen and living room. "They'll be in good hands."

Ryan stepped toward Ralph. "You should be okay, but I'm going to see if we can get a sheriff's patrol car to go by here tonight."

Ralph nodded. "I got a shotgun. We'll do just fine."

"All the same, I'll make a call." Ryan placed a supportive hand on the middle of Catherine's back as they stepped outside. The agent, a short lean woman with chin-length dark hair, had gotten out of the car.

"Agent McCloud?" She held her hand out to him as he came down the stairs. "I'm Agent Bronson from the Bozeman office."

He shook Agent Bronson's hand and then turned back toward Catherine as she came down the stairs. "This is Catherine Reed. The woman in need of protection."

He opened the back door of the car for Catherine. "It's

safest back here. Sit in the middle seat. No one can see you clearly from the outside of the car."

He didn't want to tell her that the middle back seat was the securest against a bullet finding her. She had enough to be fearful about.

Ryan settled in the front passenger seat. "Please be aware that we could be followed." The curly-haired man had to this point been persistent. He could not let his guard down.

"We will keep a close watch," said Agent Bronson.

"And I wonder if we could get the local sheriff's department to do a patrol past this farmhouse just as a precaution."

"Maybe you could make that call and let them know," said Agent Bronson.

While Ryan phoned the sheriff's department, Agent Bronson turned around and they headed up the dirt driveway. They were taking a different exit than the one they had come in on when they were being chased. This was the one they had used when they had first come to the farm.

When he checked his watch, it was nearly 2:00 a.m.

Once they were away from the light of the farmhouse, only the stars twinkling in the sky and the headlights of the agent's car lit the way.

"Any leads on the two men who came after us?"

"We've been asking around. Plenty of people saw the man with the curly hair in Lewisville. Since you couldn't give us a description of the man in the helmet, he's been a little harder to track down. That ATV rental place in Two Bits had five people rent from them yesterday. One was a woman and one was you. So we have the description of three different men. One was heavyset so we can eliminate him. That leaves two men in good shape who may be our guys. We don't think the guy would use his real name, but we are checking that trail out all the same."

"What about Victoria, any sign of her?"

"The woman you described has not surfaced in the area. We touched base with the friend she was staying with in town and there has been no additional contact."

More evidence that Victoria may have gone even deeper into hiding. The encounter with Dave probably only frightened her further. Had she given up trying to get in touch with Catherine? Ryan was glad to have the help of his fellow agents. So much more could get done.

They arrived at the turnout where the dirt road connected with the paved one. Ryan glanced around half expecting to see a car waiting in the shadows to follow them.

The drive to the safe house took about an hour. Cars got behind them from time to time. Some passed and others remained close. It did not appear that they had been followed. They were on the outskirts of the town of Bozeman, one of the larger towns in Montana and where the FBI field office was.

Agent Bronson parked in front of a two-story house with a garage. A hedge surrounded the front of the house. There were no other houses in sight, though Ryan saw lights in the distance. The houses must be on large lots.

"In order not to draw attention to this being a safe house, the locals around here think it's a vacation rental," said Agent Bronson.

She grabbed the remote sitting on the console, opened the garage and drove inside.

Ryan took in a breath as they sat in the silent, dark garage. "It's too late for me to expect an agent to take me to go get my car in Two Bits. I'll stay until daylight and make sure Catherine has extra protection."

"Thank you." Catherine's soft voice floated up from the back seat.

Agent Bronson opened the car door and turned on the light in the garage before going into the house.

Ryan got out of car and waited for Catherine so they could go in together.

"There's a bedroom downstairs and one upstairs." Agent Bronson removed her gun from the holster and placed it on the end table by the couch. "I'll be sleeping out here."

"Catherine, you take the downstairs room. I'll go upstairs." The second floor would provide him with a better view of the surrounding area. If someone did try to breach the house, he would see them coming. He intended to sleep in short intervals and keep an eye on the place from the second floor.

He was beyond exhausted, though, and he knew he needed sleep. Between him and Agent Bronson keeping watch, he hoped he could keep Catherine safe.

"I suppose I should get some sleep." Though she could collapse from fatigue, Catherine found herself still wanting to be with Ryan. "So tomorrow you'll be gone?"

"Yes, I'll need an agent to take me to get my car in Two Bits and then I'll work this case with the other agents."

Agent Bronson had wandered into the kitchen. It sounded like she was heating something up in the microwave.

"How long will I have to stay here?"

"I can't say. Until we deem your life is no longer under threat. We may need to have you transported out of the area in order to keep you from being in danger."

Her stomach tied in a knot. Being confined in the safe house was hard enough. Now Ryan was talking about her being even farther away from all that was familiar. "Are you saying I would have to go out of the state?"

"Whatever it takes to keep you hidden. I'm sorry it has to be this way," said Ryan.

They were standing three feet apart. She found herself wanting to fall into his arms. He'd been so good about keeping her safe so far, she was going to miss him. The thought made her heart ache. She wondered too if there wasn't a deeper reason why she mourned his leaving. She felt a growing affection for him beyond who he was as a lawman.

Though her sister's fear of Ryan still weighed on Catherine, Ryan had protected her and even saved her life from Dave.

"Thank you for all you've done for me. I know this is just the way it has to be." She didn't want him to go.

He studied her for a long moment. "I'm glad I got to know you, Catherine." His voice held a note of warmth. Light had come into his blue eyes. "Well, good night." He turned toward the stairway.

She grabbed his sleeve. "I mean it. I am so grateful for all you have done." She fell into his arms breathing in woodsy scent of his skin as she rested against his chest. He held her for only a moment.

He pulled away, his voice growing a little frosty. "You're welcome."

Noise from the kitchen reminded her that they were not alone. That might have been why he had pulled away so quickly. The hug had been impulsive, but she didn't regret it. She was grateful for his protection and would be sad to be separated from him.

He rubbed her forearm. "I'll do everything I can to make sure you can get back to your old life. It just might take some time."

Her skin was warm where he'd touched it. Feeling a sense of loss, she stared into the deep blue of his eyes before turning and retreating to the bedroom. The room was cozy with a floral bedspread and private bath. She took a quick shower, putting on her old clothes and then climbing under the soft covers.

She drifted off to sleep, waking hours later in darkness. The house was silent except for some creaking from the wind outside.

When she checked the clock, she'd only been asleep for a couple of hours. Her racing thoughts about what the future held had caused her to awaken. She rose from the bed and stumbled into the living room, where Agent Bronson lay on the couch.

The agent sat upright when a floorboard creaked as Catherine made her way to the kitchen. "Everything all right?"

The agent's voice didn't sound groggy at all. She must have trained herself to sleep light and wake easily when on watch.

"Yes, I just couldn't sleep. Sorry to wake you." Catherine headed toward the kitchen hoping there was milk in the fridge she could heat up. That always helped her sleep.

The refrigerator held only food that didn't spoil quickly. Some butter and eggs and half-and-half. One of the canisters on the counter had tea bags in it. She opted for some chamomile.

She found a mug and filled it with water before putting it in the microwave.

"Trouble sleeping?" Ryan stood in the doorway. His hair was ruffled, and his shirt was untucked. He looked handsome in this more relaxed state.

"Yes, I thought I'd make some tea. You want some?"

He took a seat at the table. "Nah, I'm good. What was keeping you up? You had a day worthy of a monster sleep."

She pulled the mug from the microwave when it dinged.

"All the unknowns that the future holds right now. I know I just have to trust that God is in control and that this will work out in the end."

"Yes, trusting God is sometimes all we can do."

They shared the same faith, an even deeper reason to like him. "What if we never find my sister and I have to go live somewhere far away from here?"

It occurred to her that if Dave truly did end up standing trial and going to prison that it would have been safe for her to come back to the farm once Ralph and Celeste's lease was up. But now a new menace had stolen her freedom.

She placed the tea bag in the steaming mug.

Ryan ran his hands through his hair. "I can't answer those questions. I can just do my job as best I can. Those two men will probably stay in the area for a while. With the other agents' assistance, I might be able to bring this to a close."

She took a seat facing the kitchen window that looked out on the backyard. "I wish I knew what was going on with Victoria."

"There doesn't seem to be a trace of her in this part of the world. She's either very good at hiding or she has fled somewhere else."

Catherine took a sip of her beverage enjoying the quiet companionship she felt with Ryan. Looking up from her mug, she stared out the kitchen window. Movement by the trees caught her eye. She sat up straighter.

Ryan placed his hand on hers. "Everything okay?"

"I thought I saw something out there." It was all shadows and darkness. She couldn't be sure. Plus, since she'd been on the run, everything seemed to hold a threat.

Ryan jumped to his feet as his voice grew louder. "Agent Bronson. We may have an intruder." He turned toward Catherine. "Where did you see something suspicious?"

"By that tree at the edge of the yard," said Catherine.

Within seconds, the other agent was in the doorway.

Ryan had already pulled his gun from the holster. "Agent Bronson, stay with Catherine. I'll go check outside."

"We'll lock up the house," said the other agent. "I'll turn off the light then lock the kitchen door after you go out."

"Fine," said Ryan. "I'll knock three times if I need to get back in."

Agent Bronson turned toward Catherine. "You need to be upstairs. It will be more secure up there. Come on."

Her heart was pounding by the time the female agent had locked all the doors except the one Ryan needed to use. They made it upstairs to the room that provided a view of the backyard. There was a deck surrounded by lawn and trees beyond.

"I'll need you to stay away from the window," said Agent Bronson.

Catherine retreated to a chair that was on the far side of the bedroom they were in.

"I'm going back downstairs to lock the door behind Ryan and be there in case Ryan needs to get back in quickly." Agent Bronson disappeared down the hallway.

From where she sat away from the window in the dark, Catherine couldn't see what was happening. The sound of her own breathing seemed to augment in the silence. She prayed Ryan would not be harmed and that what she had seen in the backyard was nothing.

TWELVE

Ryan stood at the kitchen door easing it open and slipping outside. He closed it with great care to keep from making noise.

He heard the lock click into place behind him as Agent Bronson relocked the door. Her primary job was to guard Catherine. She wouldn't leave her post inside the house unless absolutely necessary.

He was on his own with the potential assailant.

There were no outdoor lights on. If the guy was close, he might hear Ryan. It seemed the better option was to watch and observe rather than make his presence known. If a man was out there, he was probably armed.

Still staying close to the house, he waited for his eyes to adjust to the light. In the silence, he thought about Catherine's impulsive hug. The gesture had stirred affection in him. He was drawn to her, but he had a job to do and then he would return to Seattle. He needed to keep his focus on the investigation.

He drew his attention back to the dark yard.

The tree that Catherine had pointed to was on the edge of the yard. Nothing by the tree trunk moved nor did he hear anything that indicated a human was out there.

The backyard space opened up to a field. He looked for

the glint on metal or the outline of a car parked some distance away but could discern nothing in the near darkness.

He was about to conclude that Catherine had been mistaken when he heard a faint thud. His breath caught as he lifted his head to see better. One of the other trees appeared to have an unnaturally thick trunk.

A long moment passed while his pulse pounded in his ears. Then he saw just the faintest flutter of movement by the tree, a hand maybe.

His mouth went dry as his heart thudded.

Someone was out there.

If Ryan moved or made a noise, he'd become a target. He opted to stay close to the door and wait for the guy to do something. Sooner or later, he'd either come toward the house or seek to escape.

The wind made tree branches creak.

A single shot reverberated close to Ryan's head. His heart hammered in his chest as he took cover behind the grill on the deck, trying to see where the guy was. His gaze darted everywhere trying to separate shadows from objects.

The other guy must have moved in closer from the trees at the edge of the yard.

Slipping off the deck and crouching, he took a guess at where the shot had come from. A small hedge was the next best place to hide assuming the assailant was moving closer to the house. If he could take this guy into custody, maybe he could move the investigation forward. Still staying low, Ryan moved silently to the edge of the deck and peered above it.

He waited for what seemed a year. The wind had died down as the quiet surrounded him and all he heard was the pulsing of his own heart in his ears.

How long was this guy going to wait him out?

Then he heard the faintest swish of noise. A shadow moved from the hedge back toward one of the trees. Ryan rushed toward another tree and pressed against it, raising his gun. The guy sprinted away into the inky night.

Ryan raced after him, running into the darkness of the grassy field that surrounded the back of the house. He fired a single shot not to kill but to stop the man. He needed this man taken in alive to find out who he was and why he was after the woman he thought was Victoria.

There was enough moonlight to barely make out a silhouette. Ryan sprinted across the field. Better to try to tackle the guy than risk killing him.

He ran, drawing close enough to the other man to hear pounding footsteps. Ryan willed himself to go faster as he closed in. The whole time he ran, he was aware that the man had a gun and could turn on him and use it.

The footsteps seemed to be all around him as he leaped through the air and landed on the man's back. He saw a flash of curly hair.

The other man twisted away from Ryan and crawled on all fours, trying to get on his feet. Once upright, the curly-haired man turned suddenly and kicked Ryan, who was still not standing, hard across the jaw. The boot heel felt like it was made of iron. The blow was disorienting as pain reverberated through his jaw, head and neck.

The time it took to recover from the blow was enough for the guy to take off running again.

Despite the pain, Ryan pushed himself to his feet. He saw where the other man had dropped and left his gun.

Ryan dashed in the direction the assailant had gone.

He heard a car start up in the distance. He kept running. The glare of the red taillights filled his vision. He stopped, lifted his gun and fired a shot. The car sped away.

The man must have feared being caught and had run. That he was scared off so easily suggested he was not a seasoned assassin. That didn't mean he wouldn't come back and try again.

Ryan trudged back toward the house, stopping to pick up the dropped gun, which was now evidence. He stepped on the deck and knocked on the door three times.

Agent Bronson opened the door.

"He got away," said Ryan. "We can't stay here. It's not safe for Catherine. He might decide to come back."

"It may be that no place around here is safe for her," said Agent Bronson.

"That's what I'm afraid of. She's going to have to be moved out of the area." A development Catherine wouldn't be happy about. But he had no choice if he was going to keep her alive.

Next time the man with the curly hair came for her, he might be successful.

Catherine sat in the chair waiting in the shadows and feeling helpless. She was tempted to look out the window at the action below but knew she needed to remain out of sight. She took in a ragged breath. What if something bad happened to Ryan? She'd heard a gunshot and then minutes of quiet. Had Ryan been shot or had he stopped the intruder?

She realized then she was coming to care about him. After Dave, her heart had been so closed off to the idea that a man could be decent and not deceptive. She wiped the thoughts from her mind. She'd hadn't known him long. Hadn't her marriage to Dave proven she was a poor judge of character? She couldn't stop the feelings of attraction, but she could keep from acting on them.

His response to her quick hug had been cold. Whatever

feelings she was starting to have, he was focused on his job. Protecting her probably wasn't personal, it was professional.

She thought she heard a door open downstairs. She rose to her feet and was standing in the doorway when Agent Bronson came up the stairs and stood at the end of the hallway. She breathed a sigh of relief. Ryan was behind the female agent.

"You're okay," she said.

Ryan cleared his throat. "You were right. There was someone out there trying to breach the house. We need to get out of here."

"Ryan and I came up with a plan," Agent Bronson said. "I'm going to give the two of you a ride back to Two Bits where Ryan left his car."

"And then what?"

The two agents looked at each other and then Ryan stepped toward her. "It's not safe for you to stay in this area as long as those two guys are around and think you're Victoria."

Catherine felt like she'd been punched in the gut. "I have to go far away from here. What about the dogs? I can't leave them behind." She had a hard time even getting the words out.

Ryan reached out toward her and rubbed her shoulder. "Hopefully, it's just a short-term thing."

"But I have to stay in hiding until you find Victoria? What if she's halfway across the state by now?" She wanted to think the best of her sister, but right now it looked like Victoria had given up trying to contact her. Maybe she had taken those diamonds and had set herself up nicely in some other country, leaving Catherine to pay for deeds she had not committed.

"Let's go get my car. It's going to take some time to set something up for you anyway."

Her stomach was still tied in knots as he led her downstairs to the garage. Agent Bronson drove them back to Two Bits in the predawn light. Catherine dozed part of the way. When she opened her eyes, the sky had turned from black to gray, but the sun had not yet come up.

Agent Bronson pulled into the lot of the ATV rental place, which was still closed. The lot had a streetlight at each corner.

Ryan turned to face her in the back seat. "I think what we need to do is go to the FBI field office in Bozeman until we can set something up for you. That's the safest place for you right now."

Catherine managed a nod, though she felt numb inside.

Agent Bronson spoke up. "Once we get your car, Ryan, you can follow me if you like. I assume Catherine wants to ride with you."

"Yes, I do," said Catherine.

Ryan pushed open the car door and she followed him through the lot. As they walked toward his car, he gave her arm a reassuring squeeze.

Though she tried to see his point of view, being transported far away had put her in a dark mood. He must have picked up on it. He was tuned into her feelings even when she didn't share them.

She saw movement at the edge of the lot right before a gunshot filled the air. Catherine saw a dark-haired, broad-shouldered man lift his head above an ATV and then duck down. With the light that spilled from the streetlamp, she saw his face only for a second. That had to be the helmeted man who had chased her on the mountain. He must have been waiting here and watching, knowing that Ryan would come back for his car.

Ryan pulled her to the ground and shielded her with his

body. They were still twenty feet from his car, too far to run out in the open. They were closer to the other agent's car.

Agent Bronson had gotten out of her car and was using her open door as cover as she pulled her gun.

One of the ATVs roared to life. The man came straight toward them where they still lay on the ground. Agent Bronson fired off a shot. The man on the ATV aimed a shot in her direction. In response, she ducked down behind the car door.

After firing the shot at Agent Bronson, the man sped toward them.

The distraction was time enough for Ryan to lift Catherine off the ground, and they scrambled to get back to Agent Bronson's car before they were run over. Catherine climbed into the back seat. Ryan pulled his gun and prepared to take aim as the man sped toward the edge of the lot.

Agent Bronson shot a tire out on the ATV. The man jumped off and retreated toward the convenience store building, slipping around a corner.

Ryan stepped away from the car and chased after where the man had gone.

Catherine watched as Ryan, gun drawn, pressed his back against the building. He hesitated only for a moment before disappearing around the corner to pursue the man who had shot at them.

Catherine felt like she couldn't get a deep breath. She braced for the sounds of gunshots. Ryan could end up dead.

THIRTEEN

Ryan could hear retreating footsteps as he edged around the corner of the convenience store. Once away from the lights that illuminated the rental place, it was harder to see. He ran in the direction he thought the man had gone.

Headlights on a car parked on the other side of the street came on. Ryan got close enough to see it was the tan sedan. After watching which way the car went, he turned to get back to his own car thinking he still might be able to catch the man.

When he got back to the lot where the rentals were, Agent Bronson stood by her car still holding her gun. Catherine sat in the back seat.

"He got away in a car. I'm going to see if I can catch him," said Ryan.

Another car reached the edge of the lot and pulled into it. A bald man holding a gun got out. "What is going on here? What are you people up to? I own this place. The silent alarm went off."

Ryan and Agent Bronson both raised their hands.

"Sir, we're with the FBI," said Ryan.

"A man wanted in a case we're working on came after us on one of your ATVs," said Agent Bronson. "I shot a tire out."

The bald man lifted his chin as suspicion clouded his features. "Let me see your badges."

Both Ryan and Agent Bronson pulled out their wallets.

The bald man glanced around. "There is no law here in Two Bits. Sheriff can't get here fast enough. I have to do my own policing. I assume you're paying for the damage to my rental?"

Ryan nodded. "The bureau will take care of it."

With the delay in talking to the owner of the rental place, Ryan knew there was no chance of catching the man in the tan sedan. Though he doubted he'd give up trying to get to Catherine.

They exchanged information with the bald man. "I might as well get that tire fixed while I'm here," said the owner, who pulled out a set of keys. He walked toward a garage that was next to the convenience store.

Ryan opened the back door to Agent Bronson's car. Catherine still looked shaken. There wasn't much color in her face.

"I think it's okay for you to come out. I'm ready to take you to that field office."

"I saw his face," said Catherine.

"Do you think you would remember it if you saw a photo?" Being able to identify who the man was would be helpful in catching him.

Catherine nodded. "I think so."

"That's something we can do at the field office," he said. He reached a hand out toward her. "Do you need a moment more to calm down?"

She shook her head. "Mostly I was afraid for you, Ryan." She took his hand and got out of the car. Her skin was soft to the touch and he saw affection in her eyes.

Her response warmed him. He had to admit, he was attracted to her. He admired her courage and how loving she was toward everyone in her life, her dogs and her sister. "I can handle myself. You don't need to worry about me." He purged his voice of any affection he felt for her. No matter his feelings, he was in Montana to do a job. He'd be leaving after that. She'd been hurt enough in her life. He didn't want to get her hopes up.

Ryan escorted her over to his car and opened the passenger side door for her.

When they drove out of the lot with Agent Bronson in the lead, Ryan noticed the owner rolling a tire from his garage toward the ATV.

The drive to Bozeman took a couple of hours. The yellow lines on the road clicked by as the sun came up.

Ryan kept his eyes on the road as he followed Agent Bronson's taillights. He blinked several times and shook his head. He'd gotten only a couple hours of sleep, and it was catching up to him. Both men were proving themselves to be evasive. Getting an ID on the man that Catherine had seen would be helpful, but there must be something more they could do. "Do you suppose Victoria might get back in touch with Andrea?"

"I asked her to call me if she did," said Catherine.

He knew he had to get Catherine out of the area, but once she was no longer around, the chances of Victoria making contact would go down to zero. It was Catherine that Victoria was willing to talk to, but only if he could guarantee her safety.

"Maybe you could call Andrea and let her know that we'll be in Bozeman. I don't know for how long. It might take a day or two to secure a location far away and set up transport for you."

"You mean it might be the last chance for Victoria to come out in the open since I'm the only one she will agree to talk to?"

"Yes," said Ryan.

"I can make that call." She pulled her phone from her satchel and pressed buttons. "Andrea, no word from Victoria?…I still think she might be in touch. If she is, let her know that I am in a safe place in Bozeman." There was a long pause while Andrea spoke. "I didn't realize. I'm glad you remembered that…Okay, I know. I'm worried about her too." Catherine pressed the disconnect button.

Ryan had heard only one side of the conversation. "Didn't realize what?"

Catherine stared at her phone. "Andrea remembered that Victoria said that more than anything she wanted to mend our relationship." She put the phone away. "I need to see my sister before I'm sent into hiding somewhere far away. I need to talk to her."

Ryan picked up on the intense emotion in her voice. "You can't risk your life for that. We have to take measures to keep you safe. That means involving agents."

"I know, but there has to be a way." Her voice was barely above a whisper.

Catherine seemed to be hedging on being sent away. "Once that new location and transport is set up, you have to go." Moving Catherine out of state meant he had less of a chance of finding Victoria. But it was a sacrifice he was willing to make. While she was still here, there might be a chance to take Victoria in.

The remainder of the drive was mostly silent. Catherine seemed to be deep in thought.

Ryan stared at the road in front of him, glancing from time to time in the rearview mirror to see if they were being followed.

The field office was dark when Agent Bronson parked

in front of it. She unlocked it and let them in. The sun had come up and people were out on the street.

"Do you feel up to looking at photos? You must be tired. There's probably a couch you can crash on."

Catherine nodded. "I'd like to look at the photos first."

Ryan turned toward Agent Bronson. "Can we access the criminal database?"

"Sure, on the computer in the back room." Agent Bronson was already headed down a hallway.

She led them into a room that had two computers and file cabinets. She powered up one of the computers and typed in passwords. She gestured to Catherine and Ryan. "Have a seat, you two."

Both of them pulled up a chair.

Ryan pushed his chair closer to the computer. "Let's start by sorting through the photos and looking at known mafia associates from the Seattle area."

Agent Bronson tapped the keyboard. She pushed her chair back. "I'm going to go get us some breakfast. Other agents might show up coming off the nighttime sting operation. Wonder how it went. They were intercepting a drug shipment that was supposed to have come down through Canada."

"Would it be okay if the outside door remained locked?" Ryan hadn't seen the tan sedan behind them as they drove from Two Bits to Bozeman, but he didn't want to take any chances. Both men had shown themselves to be very good at tailing.

"It will do that automatically. I have a key card I swipe," said Agent Bronson. She tucked a strand of dark hair behind her ear and sighed. "Been a long night for all of us." She left the room.

Catherine scooted her chair closer to the computer where

the first photo had come up. "He had a really distinct face. Very square features and round, deep-set eyes."

"He had jet-black hair. I saw that much," said Ryan.

They filed through the photographs for half an hour. Agent Bronson brought them some take-out breakfast. She set the boxes down on the table. "Scrambled eggs, toast and orange juice. I hope that is to your liking."

"Anything sounds good right now," said Catherine.

Agent Bronson moved toward the door. "I'll stay in the front office until another agent shows up," she said. "As a precaution, the extra security of another agent might be a good idea given the number of attacks."

They continued to work through the photos.

"That one." Catherine pointed to the screen. "I'm pretty sure that's the guy."

Ryan tapped the keyboard to bring up information about the man in the photograph, whose name was Stephone Zander. He had known ties to the mafia. He had done prison time for kidnapping and extortion. Nothing in his rap sheet showed a connection to the jewelry industry. He must be hired muscle.

Catherine took a bite of the toast that was in her to-go box. "Now what?"

"His picture will go out to local police agencies. It will be that much harder for him to try to get to you without getting caught."

She slumped in her chair and rubbed her temples. "Let's hope they catch him."

"Are you up to trying to figure out who the man with the curly hair is?"

"Sure, if it will make it easier to catch him," she said.

They filed through the rest of the photos of men having known mafia connections, not finding anyone who looked like the man who drove the dark blue SUV. Ryan widened the search to known hitmen in the Seattle area, still not coming up with anything.

"Why don't you try to get some sleep? There's probably a couch in one of the offices," he said.

"What about you? You must be tired too."

Ryan could barely keep his eyes open, but he still had more to do to find a secure place for Catherine to be transported to. "I'll catch some sleep in a bit."

After helping Catherine find an office with a couch and tracking down a blanket for her, Ryan moved to the front office to talk to Agent Bronson. "Anyway, we can get started on setting up transport and a location for Catherine out of the area."

"That will have to wait. Agent Martin is coming in later today. He's the expert on that. Why don't you try to get some sleep? You look like you are about to fall over."

He could barely keep his eyes open. Though the thought of not seeing her again was upsetting, he felt an urgency to make sure Catherine would not be attacked again. The field office was the most secure place right now with the extra support from Agent Bronson and other agents coming in. Even with that, he had to keep in mind that if they had been followed to the safe house, they might have been followed to the field office as well.

Turning toward the wall, he settled in on the couch in the main office while Agent Bronson worked on her computer. He fell into a restless sleep.

Catherine awoke to the sound of her phone buzzing. The number was Andrea's. Her heart squeezed tight as she shook the fog of a deep sleep off.

She had slept for hours. It had to be well after lunchtime. She pressed the connect button. "Hello, Andrea."

"Victoria called me again from a different number." Andrea's voice was high-pitched.

Catherine threw off the blanket and sat up on the couch. "What did she say?"

"I told her you were in Bozeman. She is too."

"Does she want me to meet her somewhere?"

"There's a coffee shop downtown called the Mountain Brew," said Andrea.

"What time?"

"In an hour. Come alone. Catherine, she sounds so afraid," said Andrea.

"Andrea, thank you for letting me know she called. Has it been safe for you? That man with the curly hair hasn't come back, has he?"

"If he's come back, I haven't seen him. The police have been really good about driving by the house several times a day. It's a small town. My neighbors all know what he looks like. If he did come by, there would be a call to the police right away. I'm not worried for my safety anymore."

"That's good to hear." The news that Andrea was safe made Catherine breathe a sigh of relief, but it also indicated that the curly-haired man was probably focused on tracking her down.

"Do let me know what happens with Victoria. I think of her as the daughter I never had."

"As soon as I know what is going on, I'll be in touch." Her heart raced as she pressed the disconnect button and rose from the couch.

She hurried into the front office where Ryan was sitting at a computer with another agent who wasn't Agent Bronson. A man with salt-and-pepper hair and a mustache sat behind the desk.

Ryan shifted in his chair. "Catherine, this is Agent Martin."

Catherine nodded. She still gripped her phone in her hand.

"Everything okay? Did you get some sleep?"

There was no time for small talk. "Andrea called. Victoria got in contact with her again. She wants to meet me here in Bozeman in an hour."

Ryan rose to his feet and began to pace, running his hands through his hair. "This is good but kind of a tight timeline. This time, we go by the book. We have a team of agents watching you. I'm not taking a chance of her getting away again or you being harmed. Those two men are still out there."

"She'll recognize you." Catherine felt a tightening in her stomach. She might lose her sister forever if she broke trust between them.

Ryan rose to his feet. "I'll stay out of sight. The other agents will be set up to look like coffee shop patrons."

She didn't want to break her word to Victoria, but Ryan was right. She needed the protection. At the same time, she couldn't take the chance that Victoria would bolt before she could find out what was going on with her. "You have to give me a chance to talk to Victoria, though. To hear her side of the story." She still wanted to believe that her sister was innocent. "You can't just swoop in and arrest her."

"I don't want to arrest her unless she has broken the law. She needs to be taken in for questioning," said Ryan. "We'll need to listen in on the conversation."

"No, I don't want to do anything to break her trust. The other agents are there just to protect me. They don't make a move on her unless she tries to run away. This might be the last time she tries to get in touch with me. I don't want to risk her not talking to me. I don't want to lose my sister forever."

Ryan glanced at Agent Martin, who shrugged.

"I'm not sure we even have time to get a surveillance van in place and set her up with a wire," said Agent Martin.

"This whole thing is going to be rushed," said Ryan. "Victoria is skittish. We can't risk not making contact."

"Yes, it would be nice to have more time to get the equipment in place," said Agent Martin. "And it puts Catherine at risk if we can't hear the conversation."

"My sister is not going to hurt me, and I'll be in a public place." She knew she was at odds with Ryan once again. "Look, I know you have an obligation to take her in, but can't we win her trust before we do that? Maybe she's innocent and has a good reason why she's gone into hiding. I'm the one she's willing to talk to."

Ryan studied her for a long moment then turned back toward Agent Martin. "We don't have much time. How many agents can we get on this?"

"Two right away. Myself. Agent Bronson has had a chance at a little rest. We can pull her in."

"That will have to do," said Ryan. "You both need to be in place before the meeting time."

"It doesn't give us much time." Agent Martin was on his feet. "We won't be able to obtain much of an idea of the layout of the place."

"Let's get over there and find out as much as we can. Can you and Agent Bronson be wired up so I can hear you?"

"There is time for that. I'll grab the equipment."

Ryan grabbed his holster that held his gun and put his jacket on over it. "I will remain outside in my vehicle out of sight, but if there is any danger to Catherine, I need to be called in."

"I'll give Agent Bronson a call. Let's get this rolling." Agent Martin picked up the office phone and wandered to the corner of the desk with his back turned.

The conversation between the two men had made her even more nervous.

Ryan turned back to face her. "We won't put a wire on you, but one of the agents will sit close enough to hear the conversation. If your sister admits to taking those diamonds or any other crime, we have to take her in."

Catherine nodded. "Not until I've spoken to her. She has to know I'm on her side." They had come to a compromise. It was the best they could do under the circumstances.

Agent Martin hung up the phone. "Agent Bronson is driving over to the coffee shop right now to try and get as much of an idea of the situation as she can. I need to get some clothes that make me look less like an FBI agent and more like someone who hangs out in a coffee shop. I think I have a shirt in the back office. I can meet you there."

"Great, Catherine and I will head over in my car," said Ryan. "I want to see what we're dealing with in relationship to the surrounding buildings. Let me know when the two of you are in place and I'll send Catherine in."

The speed at which the plan was being thrown together made Catherine anxious. Victoria had probably intended to make the meeting happen quickly so Ryan wouldn't have time to set up elaborate surveillance. "What if Victoria sees you parked on the street?"

"I won't get out of the car, but I'm going to stay as close as I can, Catherine. I'll park where I can watch the street and the entrance." Ryan squeezed her upper arm. His touch sent a wave of calm through her. "What I'm asking you to do is dangerous. I want to do everything to guarantee your safety."

"This was my decision… I know what I'm getting myself into."

Agent Martin disappeared in a back room and returned holding three boxes that must contain the communication equipment. He handed one of the boxes to Ryan. He was wearing a different shirt that looked much more casual than the button-down he'd had on.

"Let's get rolling. We don't have much time."

Agent Martin followed them out to the parking lot after locking the door of the field office.

Butterflies fluttered in Catherine's stomach as she got into Ryan's car. Ryan typed the name of the coffee shop into his GPS and drove across town. The coffee shop was in the busy downtown area but on a side street.

Traffic was congested. Downtown Bozeman had several multistoried parking garages, as well as tall buildings that blocked the view. The amount of people, cars and tall buildings made the area seem claustrophobic.

Catherine glanced around thinking she might see the tan sedan or the blue SUV.

"If you are looking for them, they may have switched cars by now," said Ryan. "If they were smart, that is what they would do, and so far, both these men have proven themselves to be pretty savvy."

She took in a deep breath to try to quell the rising fear she felt. Ryan drove around the block and found the coffee shop on a corner next to a place that sold outdoor clothing and fishing gear. It had large windows on two sides.

Victoria must have chosen such a busy place for a reason. Maybe it was easier to hide in a crowd. Every time the fear rose up, Catherine reminded herself of what Andrea had told her about Victoria wanting more than anything to reconcile with her.

Ryan drove several blocks away from the coffee shop, studying all the streets that surrounded the area. He returned to the street where the coffee shop was and circled the block until a parking space across the street and one block from the coffee shop opened up.

"This is as close as I can get you," said Ryan. "I'll have a view of the storefront and the surrounding shops from here."

They still had ten minutes before the meeting time. Ryan opened the box that Agent Martin had given him and put a headset on. He spoke into the microphone. "Agents Bronson and Martin, give me your location." He listened for a moment and then turned toward her. "They're both in place. You need to find a spot close to where one of them is seated."

"I'll do my best." She studied the people on the sidewalk thinking she might see one of the two men.

"You ready for this?" Ryan had unbuttoned his jacket, so he had quick access to his gun. "I'll be watching. I'll alert the agents if I see anything amiss on the street."

"I'm ready." She pressed her head against the seat, closed her eyes and said a quick prayer.

By the time Catherine pushed open the car door and stepped out onto the sidewalk, her heart was pounding hard.

FOURTEEN

Though it was a short walk to the coffee shop, Catherine could feel her legs turn to cooked noodles as she made her way up the street. She glanced back at the car where Ryan was before reaching for the door to the coffee shop. He was slumped low in the seat.

Inside, a cacophony of noises greeted her, coffee orders being shouted and conversation rising and falling in intensity.

She spotted Agent Bronson right away sitting in front of a laptop typing. There were no empty seats around her. The place was full to capacity. Two people were in front of her waiting to make their coffee orders. She studied the room again while she waited in line, finally locating Agent Martin in the middle of the room holding a book and wearing a flannel shirt.

Her heart was still racing as she stepped to order a drink that could be made quickly, an Americano. Again, she studied the room, trying not to stare while registering each face. There were two women with their backs to the front door. It seemed if Victoria had come early, she would have chosen a spot with a view of the entrance.

Agent Martin lifted his head in slight recognition but did not look directly at her.

The barista handed her the coffee and she moved over to the counter where she could put in sugar and cream while still watching the room, her stomach tied in knots.

A table opened up next to Agent Martin, and she hurried toward it before it was taken. Her back was to Agent Martin, but she had a view of the entrance to the coffee shop.

A woman too old to be Victoria stepped into the shop and glanced around.

Catherine took a sip of her coffee, grateful that the cream had cooled it down. All the tables around her were full and most contained at least two people in conversation.

An eruption took place several tables over. A woman raised her voice at the man she was with and stomped toward the door, tossing her coffee cup in the garbage on the way out.

Catherine had taken her eyes off the door for only a second. Had she missed Victoria coming into the place? A woman with a long coat stood in line to order with her back to Catherine. She was tall like Victoria.

Agent Martin, still holding his book, turned sideways in his chair and whispered under his breath. "You're fine. I haven't seen her yet."

She took several long, slow sips of her coffee and then checked the time on her phone. Victoria was two minutes past the agreed-upon meeting time.

A man wearing a baseball hat loitered outside on the sidewalk with his back to the shop windows. Several people passed by, visible through the big windows.

Minutes passed. A knot of tension formed at the back of Catherine's neck. She took another sip of her coffee.

Victoria was late.

There were plenty of reasons why she might be delayed. Some benign, like she couldn't find a parking space, and others more nefarious, like she'd run into one of the two men who were after her or she'd simply decided it was too dangerous to show up.

Catherine would wait here an hour if that's what it took to finally talk to her sister.

Several people came into the shop at once, a mother with a teen daughter, a woman with long, dark hair and an older couple. All moved to stand in the line to order. Catherine watched the woman with the dark hair wondering if Victoria had worn a wig to disguise who she was. The woman with the dark hair was turned away from Catherine. She couldn't see her face.

When Catherine drew her attention back to what was going on in the room, another woman who had been sitting at the back of the shop reading was walking toward her. The woman didn't look anything like Victoria.

Then she made momentary eye contact, looking away quickly.

It was Victoria, but it didn't look like Victoria. Only the eyes gave her away. She'd done something with makeup to make her face look different and she was wearing a blond wig. She must have extra clothes on beneath her rust-colored coat to make herself look heavier.

Catherine's heart skipped a beat as she sat up straighter.

Victoria had been waiting and watching at the back of the coffee shop this whole time, hidden behind a book.

A moment of recognition passed between the two sisters. Victoria was within six feet of her table when she glanced toward the door. A look of fear crossed her features and she bolted toward the *employee only* exit.

Catherine saw then what had frightened her twin. The man in the baseball cap standing outside turned slightly. It was the curly-haired man. His hair was hidden under the hat. He stared through the windows, making eye contact with Catherine. Of course, it was her he would come after. Victoria didn't even look like Victoria.

Through the window, she saw him reaching for the door.

"The man in the baseball cap is outside!" Catherine called to Agent Martin as she ran after Victoria.

Agent Martin bolted to his feet and headed toward the entrance just as the man in the baseball cap opened the door. He turned around when Agent Martin came toward him.

Catherine ran behind the counter where Victoria had gone. She hurried down a short hallway and pushed through the door, stepping out into an alley. She didn't see her sister anywhere. Which way had she gone? Victoria would seek escape on the street that was opposite of where the curly-haired man had been.

Catherine hurried in that direction. When she looked over her shoulder, Agent Bronson had just stepped out in the alley. Catherine turned a corner and reached a busy street, scanning the crowds and groups of people. She saw her sister's rust-colored coat about a block away almost hidden by a cluster of four people walking close together.

Catherine ran to catch up with her sister, pushing past people. As she passed another alley, a hand went over her mouth and she was pulled backward. She was dragged deeper into the alley.

A voice whispered in her ear, "You're going to tell me where those diamonds are one way or another."

She twisted her body trying to get away. Her hand went up to her mouth. She scratched the man's hand, hoping to break free of his grip on her mouth so she could cry out. She could just see the man's dark hair and square jaw in her peripheral vision. This was not the curly-haired man but Stephone Zander, the man with ties to the mafia.

Out on the busy street, she saw Agent Bronson hurry by with her attention not on the alley but on the street filled with people.

Catherine felt herself being hauled deeper into the alley where the tan sedan was parked partially hidden behind a dumpster. The man pulled a scarf out with one hand while keeping his arm suctioned around her waist. She had only a moment to cry out while the man sought to tie the scarf on her mouth.

"Help." She was breathless from the struggle and her words sounded weak as if they had fallen on the ground at her feet.

Her hands were free. She turned and hit him in the stomach twice. The man grunted but otherwise seemed unfazed from the blows as he swung her around, jerking one hand behind her and then grabbing the other and twisting wire around her hands.

He swung open the back door of the car and pushed her stomach first onto the back seat. She heard a door slam as she struggled to get into a sitting position, which was impossible because of the restraints on her hands.

The car rolled forward up the alley. Her heart pounded from intense fear. The gag made it hard to get a breath and the wires dug into her wrist every time she moved. Her stomach pressed against the hard vinyl of the seat.

He must be taking her somewhere to question her. He would never believe that she wasn't Victoria. When she couldn't tell him where the diamonds were, would he just kill her?

Ryan knew something was wrong when Agent Martin emerged from the coffee shop glancing up and down the street, and then raced up the block apparently in pursuit of someone.

Before Ryan could speak through the headset to ask what was going on, Agent Bronson's voice came across the line. "I've lost Catherine. I'm not sure why she rushed out of the coffee shop."

Adrenaline surged through his body as he sat up a little straighter. Catherine was in danger. "Where are you? Did Victoria even show up?"

"I'm on the other side of the street, the back side of the coffee shop." Agent Bronson sounded like she was out of breath and running. "Catherine just disappeared. Victoria never entered the shop, but there was a woman who caused a ruckus right before Catherine ran out."

"I'll help you look for her." He moved to open his door.

Agent Bronson's voice came through his headset. "I backtracked to an alley. I just saw a tan sedan head up the alley toward your street."

Even before Agent Bronson had completed her sentence, Ryan saw the car emerge from the alley onto the street where he was parked.

"I'm in pursuit," said Ryan. His chest squeezed tight. Was Catherine in that car?

"I'm going to search the area some more just in case it's not our suspect's car," said Agent Bronson.

He took his hand off the door handle. The sedan was stopped at a red light. Ryan had to wait while several cars rolled by on the street before he could pull out. Once he was on the street, there was only two cars between him and the tan sedan. The light was still red.

"Agent Bronson, talk to me. Are you sure Victoria didn't show up?"

"Everything happened so fast. A woman who might have

been Victoria left by the employee entrance, but she never spoke to Catherine. It didn't look like her." Agent Bronson still sounded like she was moving at a good pace as her words came between breaths. "I was watching the entrance the whole time."

The light turned green.

Ryan pressed the gas. Downtown traffic was so congested they moved at a snail's pace. The tan sedan had to stop to allow another car to back into a parking space.

Would the man in the sedan recognize Ryan's car?

Agent's Martin's voice came through the headset. It sounded like he was running. "In pursuit of a man who matches the description you gave of the second man who came after Catherine."

Agent Bronson spoke up. "Where are you?"

"Corner of Wilson and Olive. Suspect is still on foot."

"I'll try to get to you," said Agent Bronson.

"Suspect has on gray pants and coat."

He hoped the agents would be able to capture the curly-haired man.

The sedan rolled forward. He was grateful the truck that was now between him and the sedan partially shielded him from view. The cars sped up as they got away from the congestion of downtown.

The truck turned off on a different street as they reached the edge of town. The sedan turned at the next street where a sign indicated there was a park and that this was the turn-off to get to the hospital.

Ryan hung back but kept the car in view, grateful when another car turned from a side street to slip in between them. He watched as the sedan's turn signal blinked.

When he turned onto the same street, he lost sight of the sedan. He was sure it had turned into the area where the park was. Ryan hit his turn signal. The area was huge and contained a dog park and a baseball field where a game was going on. The parking lot by the baseball field was full. Several cars circled the lot looking for an open space.

His attention was drawn at first to the street closest to the parking lot, but he didn't see the sedan speeding away. He rolled through the lot, stopping for people to cross to get to their cars. Three boys in baseball uniforms meandered through the lot.

He caught sight of the tan sedan parked illegally several rows away.

Ryan drove toward the vehicle. He stopped when he could see into the driver's side window. No one was visible behind the wheel. He pulled his weapon and got out of the car, approaching slowly. A man leaving the game carrying baseball equipment stopped and then ducked behind a car when he saw Ryan with the gun. Several other people stared and remained at a distance.

Ryan drew nearer to the sedan. No one was ducked down in the front seat. When he stared in the back seat, he saw Catherine laying on her stomach with bound hands.

His heart lurched at the sight of her so vulnerable. He pushed away images of the bad things that could have happened to her.

He swung open the door. "It's all right. I'm here."

He reached in and untwisted the wire around her wrists.

Catherine turned on her side and then sat up. She lifted her hand to remove the gag from her mouth. "I was so afraid." He reached out toward her when her eyes watered. Feeling a rush of gratitude, he gathered her into his arms. She was safe for now.

Ryan lifted her to her feet and held her. She was still trembling from fear. He drew her close hoping to comfort her. He breathed in the scent of her perfume relishing the moment.

He glanced around, not seeing any sign of the man with the dark hair. Stephone Zander must have realized he was about to be caught and had fled. He'd probably left the car behind when he saw that it made him too easy to catch. One way or another, he'd acquire another car.

Ryan embraced Catherine until she calmed and wasn't shaking so badly. He relished being able to hold her in his arms, grateful he could ease the terror she'd suffered just by being close to her.

She pulled away and gazed up at him. His hand touched her cheek and she closed her eyes. "I'm so glad you came for me." She opened her eyes. Her gaze was magnetic.

As he looked into her brown eyes, he found himself wanting to kiss her. The fact that she could have died at Zander's hands made him realize how much he cared about her. "I only want you to be safe." His throat tightened and his voice broke when he spoke. "I don't want anything bad to happen to you."

She didn't answer right away, just kept looking at him.

She shook her head. "Thanks to you, he didn't hurt me. He wanted to know where the diamonds were, and he said he'd find out one way or another." Her voice still held a tremor. "I'm pretty sure he would have killed me no matter what."

The thought made him hug her even tighter. "I won't let that happen."

He'd have to make arrangements for the tan sedan to be taken in for evidence. Also, he wondered what had happened with Agents Bronson and Martin and the other suspect, but for now, all he wanted was to hold Catherine.

He waited until she pulled away. "If you hadn't come for me, who knows what would have happened."

He met her gaze and was nourished by the affection he saw in her eyes. "But I did come for you. You're safe now."

She studied him for a long moment. Her hand fluttered to his cheek.

"Let's get you back to the car." He wrapped an arm around her back and led her the short distance to his car.

He opened the door for her. Again, he surveyed the area, aware that the man might be hiding, waiting for an opportunity to come at them. He couldn't have gotten far on foot.

He called the police and gave a description of Zander and then made the call to see that the sedan was towed and taken in for evidence.

Just as he started the car, Agent Bronson's voice came across the line. "Suspect is in custody. We're taking him back to the field office for questioning."

"Hold on." He touched his headset. "Wait until I can get there. I need to be present when he's questioned. This is our first big break."

"We can do that," said Agent Bronson.

"I'll get there as fast as I can. I have Catherine. She's safe. Stephone Zander is still at large." Ryan turned to face Catherine. "They caught the other guy. The man with the curly hair."

Relief spread across her face. "Maybe now we will get some answers."

"Let's get back to the field office." Ryan said.

People were still walking through the parking lot and cars continued to circle looking for a space. He eased through the lot, stopping to let pedestrians get by. Ryan was almost to the edge of the lot when he saw a man pop up between cars and lift a gun to fire it.

He swerved, nearly hitting a parked car. The shot shattered the window of a parked car.

"Get down," he shouted.

Catherine bent forward in her seat.

People ran away from where Zander was toward the ball field.

More than anything Ryan wanted to take this man into custody, but he couldn't risk Catherine's safety. He sped away through the lot and out onto the road.

The police were probably on their way, but he had a feeling Zander would be long gone by then.

FIFTEEN

As they drove through town, Catherine still had not stopped shaking. She had been face-to-face with the man who wanted to kill her. The man who thought she was Victoria.

Ryan's voice filled with compassion when he glanced over at her. "I know that was scary. I'll get you to the field office as fast as I can."

She knew there was no true secure place for her. The only thing that had helped calm her was being held by Ryan. And now, the sound of his voice was a soothing balm. "I can't believe how close I was to being able to talk to my sister in that coffee shop."

"What happened back at the coffee shop anyway? Agent Bronson wasn't even sure. She said Victoria never came through the front door."

"Victoria was sitting at the back of the shop before we even got there. She changed her appearance. She even walked different. I wouldn't have recognized her if she hadn't looked right at me."

"Let me guess," said Ryan. "She got scared away by the suspect we now have in custody."

"Yes, she must have seen him through the window. She changed her appearance so much. I don't think anyone would have realized it was her but me."

They drove through town and arrived at the field office.

Ryan parked close to the office door. "Stay in the vehicle. I'll come around and get you."

He pushed open his door and ran around to her side of the car. When he opened her car door, he reached out and pressed his hand against her cheek. "I know this is a lot to deal with."

His touch settled her frayed nerves. She felt a sense of peace when she looked into his blue eyes and appreciated that he was tuned in to her emotional state.

He wrapped an arm around her back and escorted her to the door of the field office. Inside, Agent Bronson waited in the reception area.

"Agent Martin is with the suspect in the interrogation room," said Agent Bronson.

"Let me make sure Catherine is okay." He turned to face her. "Do you want a drink of water or something?"

"I'll be fine," said Catherine. "Go question this guy. I want to know who he is and why he came looking for Victoria."

"Agent Bronson, can you escort Catherine to the back room where that couch is? After we're done questioning this man, local law enforcement will take him into custody to hold him for us."

"I can make that arrangement and help Catherine," said Agent Bronson.

"I want Catherine hidden away. There is no reason for him to get a look at her."

It touched her heart that Ryan was being so protective of her.

He patted her arm. "Agent Bronson will take care of you." She caught the flash of affection in his eyes before he hurried down a hallway.

Agent Bronson rose from the chair she'd been sitting in. "There's a room back down the other hallway."

Catherine followed her along a hallway into a room that must function as the break room. It had a couch and table with a coffeepot on it. A water cooler sat in the other corner of the room.

"Are you sure you don't want some coffee or something?"

Catherine sat down on the couch. "My stomach is too upset to drink anything. Maybe in a while."

Agent Bronson moved toward the door. "I'll leave you alone then."

Catherine half rose from the couch. "Could you ask Ryan to come talk to me when he's done to let me know what that man said?"

"Sure. Once they have his name, I'll look to see if he has a record. I'll just be outside in the front office if you need anything. You're safe here. The doors lock automatically. Only agents have the key card that opens them." Agent Bronson left, closing the door partway.

The agent's words hung in the air. A reminder that one man might be in custody but the other was still out there.

As she sat alone in the room, Catherine realized she had not had time to process all that had happened. She felt a sense of despair that she'd come so close to being able to know why Victoria wanted to talk to her.

What had she seen in her sister's eyes? A terror so deep it had made her run before she could talk to Catherine? Or was it guilt? Even if she had taken the diamonds, Victoria had chosen to stay in the area for some reason. Was it just about reconciling with her?

As the minutes ticked by, she thought too of the dogs. She missed Betty and was just getting to know Liz. Ryan hadn't brought up taking her out of the area again, but it was probably the next thing that was going to happen. The thought of leaving the dogs behind, even though she knew they were in good hands, caused her heart to ache.

If only Victoria would try one more time to contact her.

She rose from her seat and paced, stopping to fill a cup at the water cooler and take a few sips even though her stomach was still doing somersaults.

Everything was so up in the air. Though she saw the reason for it, she didn't want to be whisked out of state to some safe location. She took another sip of water. An idea occurred to her. Victoria had been the one to make contact through Andrea. What if she sent a message to her sister and set up a meeting place? She wasn't sure if that would even work. Victoria may have gotten rid of the phone she used to call Andrea by now. Would Ryan back her idea?

She slumped back down on the couch. It might not even work. She didn't want to go into hiding far away from Montana. The only way to prevent that was to get this resolved.

Maybe Ryan would learn something by questioning the suspect that would change everything. That felt like a very faint hope, though. She had to do something.

Ryan and Agent Martin sat across the table from the man who had tried to kill Catherine more than once. The curly hair and boyish face made him look more like a pledge for a fraternity than an assassin.

They had agreed before entering the room that Ryan would lead the questioning. He had had only a few minutes to come up with a strategy. He'd decided not to tell the man that he was stalking the wrong woman.

That gave Victoria a degree of safety and his goal all along had been to make contact with Victoria. Catherine would be taken out of state soon enough to a safe place.

Getting information out of this man was the only lead Ryan had right now.

Ryan studied the man long enough to make him uncomfortable. They'd taken the man's wallet from him when he'd been handcuffed. Ryan put the wallet on the table. It had contained no ID.

"Why don't we start with your name, since you seem to lack anything in that wallet that might tell me who you are."

The man stared at Ryan but did not reply. His mouth drew into a tight line as he lifted his chin slightly.

"We'll figure out your identity soon enough." From the chair where he sat, Agent Martin leaned toward the suspect. "Once we get a set of fingerprints. It will be easy enough to find out who you are if you have any kind of a record."

The man's eye twitched, but he still didn't say anything.

"Do you want to tell me why you went after the woman in the coffee shop and about your previous attempts to come after her and me?"

The man gazed at the ceiling for a long moment before letting out a breath. He stared at Ryan with eyes the color of dark chocolate. "I'm going to jail no matter what, right?"

"Stalking, attempted murder, just to name a few of the charges," said Ryan.

Ryan's words caused another nervous eye twitch from the man. He placed his cuffed hands on the table. "I'm not from around here. I was hired by a guy in Seattle to find Victoria Stevenson and kill her. That's all I know."

"Who hired you?"

The man stared at the ceiling again then looked off to the side. "I never met the guy. All the negotiations were done through a third party and via texting." It seemed the man had given up the information a little too easily, which made Ryan suspicious if he was telling everything he knew.

Ryan stood up so he towered over the suspect. "You never saw the man who paid you to kill Victoria?"

"No," said the man with the curly hair.

Again, something wasn't ringing true. The man's body language, looking off to one side, emphasizing each word, also suggested that he was not being forthright. "Victoria knew who you were. She recognized you when you came after her in Lewisville."

The man's face blanched as he raised his eyebrows. The information had surprised him. His Adam's apple moved up and down. "Okay, let's just say that I have had some dealings with people who work in the gem industry. Maybe she knew me from there."

Ryan detected the slight crack in the man's voice, a sign of fear.

Agent Martin piped up. "I have a feeling you're not telling us everything you know."

The man shrugged.

Ryan took another tack, hoping it would lead to more explicit information. "How did you find Victoria in Lewisville? That couldn't have been easy." He hoped the flattery would make the man open up a little more. He sat back down in his chair.

"I knew her first and last name. She'd never been married or so the man who hired me said. There had been a Victoria Stevenson born in Lewisville. People on the run often return to what is familiar. I took a chance and came out here."

"But you're saying you never had contact with the man who hired you, yet he gave you information about Victoria's marital status?" Ryan would buy that this man was paid to go after Victoria, but he probably knew who had hired him and maybe even was afraid of him.

The man's jaw grew tight and then he licked his lips. "That kind of info could come through a text. I had a picture of Victoria and basic specs on her."

It was clear the man was not going to budge on who had hired him. "Tell you what." Ryan slapped his hand on the table. "We're going to escort you down to the local police station for safekeeping. They'll fingerprint you while you're there."

The man hung his head. "My name is George Willis since you're going to find out anyway."

"We'll verify that soon enough." Agent Martin rose to his feet and walked around to the side of the table where the suspect was. "Scoot your chair back and get to your feet." The agent looked at Ryan. "I'll take him in."

"Wait just a minute," said Ryan. "I need to talk to you outside."

They left the suspect in the room. Once the door was closed, Ryan leaned close to Agent Martin. "We need to monitor George's calls once he's in jail. He may try to make contact with the man who hired him."

"Got it. I'll let the local police know."

They stepped back into the room where George sat staring at the wall.

Ryan waited in the room while Agent Martin escorted the suspect out of the building. They had a man in custody, but whoever had hired him was still out there. He left the interrogation room and found Agent Bronson in the front office.

"We need to work on safe transport and a secure location for Catherine."

Agent Bronson swiveled in her chair. "That takes a day or two to set something that complicated up. Agent Martin will take care of it when he gets a moment."

"In the meantime, let's find her a temporary safe location," said Ryan. "Can you help with protection duty?"

Agent Bronson pushed herself toward the keyboard on the desk. "I'll see what I can do."

"I have a better idea," Catherine's voice came from behind him. She had walked up the hallway.

Ryan turned to face her. "What are you talking about?"

"Up until now, we let my sister be the one to make contact and set up the meetings. It's clear she wants to talk to me. What if we set something up by communicating to her through Andrea?"

"Catherine, you were kidnapped the last time you tried to meet your sister," Ryan said. "I think it's just too risky."

"I want this resolved."

"The man we took into custody is a hired assassin. That means there is someone behind him. I suspect it's the other player in the illegal gem game and that Victoria was able to identify him. It would explain why she was gathering evidence with the figurines and photos. That's why he wants her dead."

Catherine's voice dropped half an octave. "I didn't realize." She stared at the carpet for a moment. Then she lifted her chin and locked him into her gaze. "You came to Montana to find my sister. I'm the only reason she was willing to take a risk and come out of hiding. I'm the best bait for getting my sister to come out in the open."

Ryan was in turmoil over his desire to complete his mission and his need to keep Catherine from harm. "I think we had better not risk it."

"I want to help my sister and you want to make contact with her." Catherine stepped toward him. "I want this to be over. Do you even have a next move if we can't bring my sister out into the open?"

"The suspect has given us his name. We can work that angle to figure out who might have hired him." Catherine was right. The stronger lead would be to take in Victoria and find out what she knew.

"This won't be over quickly if you send me to another state. For how long will I be separated from the dogs and the wilderness I love? Days? Months?" Her voice quivered. "Years?"

Her words were like a knife to his heart. "I can't say." He didn't want to confine her and take her away from everything that mattered to her. Everything that made her feel alive. But he didn't want to put her in danger again.

"Please," said Catherine.

"It's settled, Catherine. You need to be under protection and not out in the open." All the good feelings between them seemed to vaporize in her wanting to go against his judgment. Why couldn't she see, he cared about her and wanted to keep her safe?

SIXTEEN

Catherine collapsed in one of the plush chairs in the reception area of the field office trying to fight off the disappointment she felt over Ryan putting his foot down about her plan. "What if my sister tries to set up another meeting?"

"It didn't work last time and you could have died. We need a new strategy." There was a note of irritation in Ryan's voice, and she could feel the tension between them.

She wasn't going to give up on her idea, but maybe it would be best to back off for now.

Agent Bronson continued to type on the keyboard. "What if we take Catherine back to the safe house she was at before? The man who came after her there is in custody now. Otherwise, we're looking at a long drive and exposure."

Ryan stepped toward Agent Bronson. "I guess that might be our best option in the short term. How fast can we put that in place?"

"The house is empty. We just need to drive there," said Agent Bronson.

"Two vehicles. Two of us protecting her." Ryan glanced in Catherine's direction. "Does that work for you?"

"Since when do you care about what I want?" She rose from the chair. She could not suppress her irritation.

"I'm trying to make the best decision I can here, Catherine," he said.

Agent Bronson wiggled in her chair, clearly uncomfortable with the interaction. "Tell you what. Why don't I go get the three of us something to eat?" She rose from her chair and headed toward the door.

Once she was outside, Ryan made sure the door was locked.

Catherine retreated to the back room and sat down on the couch.

A moment later, Ryan stood in the doorway. "Hey." He stepped into the room and sat down beside her on the couch. "Look, I know you're not happy with this. But I have a judgment call to make."

"It makes your investigation harder to put me in hiding far away, and it makes my life more miserable."

"I'm only thinking of your safety," he said.

"I can see that. But I'm telling you, I'm willing to take the risk to bring this to an end."

"Please, Catherine. You matter to me."

His words were tinged with an unexpected intensity and she met his gaze, seeing deep affection in his eyes. The seconds of connection were unexpected. She studied him for a long moment, taking in the crease between his eyebrows that suggested anguish. She felt like she was seeing him for the first time. Whatever Victoria thought of him, she saw that he was a good agent trying to do the right thing. He mattered to her too. "Guess we are at an impasse." Her words were soft and without ire.

Her gaze fell to the floor and then she looked at him again, taken in by his blue eyes and the strong jawline.

"I guess we are. I only wish that you would trust me in the decisions I make." He rose to his feet and left the room.

She had not failed to pick up on the note of hurt in his voice.

Once he stepped outside the room, Ryan was grateful that Agent Bronson had returned with three to-go containers. He placed one down and brought the other to Catherine.

She took it from him. "It smells good."

There was still tension between them. Why couldn't she see that he only had her best interest in mind? It hurt his ability to move the investigation forward to take her out of the equation, and yet he was willing to do it.

He chose to eat in the front office with Agent Bronson. "How did you get this so quickly?"

"There's a hamburger joint just across the street."

He bit into his burger and ate a couple of fries. He was almost done with his meal when Catherine emerged from the back room and took a seat in one of the chairs. He didn't want to talk any more about what needed to happen to keep Catherine safe.

He didn't want to think about Catherine not backing his decision. He knew it was hard for her, but why couldn't she see that his choosing to put her in protective custody was a sacrifice for him?

From the moment he'd met Catherine, he'd been fighting to win her trust. Because of the cloud of Victoria's *no police* order. Because of her ex-husband's brutality. Things that had nothing to do with who he was.

He was grateful when his phone rang. He needed a break from his own thoughts.

Agent Martin. He pressed the connect button on his phone. "Agent McCloud. What's up?"

"You were right. George made a call almost right away. Seattle area code. The guy hung up pretty quickly. Probably suspected the call was monitored. We're trying to trace it all the same and maybe get an ID on who George is in contact with."

"That is progress." He wondered, though, if the arrest of George Willis wouldn't bring the man from Seattle to Montana or another hired assassin. It wasn't the end of trouble to have George in custody. "Has he given any other information?"

"No, he's being pretty tight-lipped. We were able to pull up his record. Lot of petty theft. No violent crime."

"So he's probably not a professional hitman," said Ryan. "Any known mafia connections?"

"No. We also got hold of his work records. He worked briefly as a clerk in a jewelry store in Seattle. We'll contact his former employer."

"Chances are he's also done things under the table as well. That would more likely be who hired him."

"True," said Agent Martin. "If we can't get an ID on the phone call, we will follow any leads on who he might have known in Seattle who could have hired him."

"Let's hope that brings in whoever he's working for." If they could get the man who had sent George, Catherine would be that much safer.

"I should be back at the office within ten minutes."

"Okay, Agent Bronson and I are going to transport Catherine to the safe house. I'm sure Bronson would like to be relieved of protection duty at some point if you can come by or spare another agent."

Catherine rose from her chair at the mention of the safe house. She wandered through the front office and then retreated to the back room again.

"We'll see what we can work out," said Agent Martin.

He said goodbye and pressed the disconnect button.

The office phone rang. Agent Bronson stepped to the desk to take the call. She spoke in hushed tones, her answers short and her words clipped. She hung up.

"That was the agent in charge of this drug bust case. We may have caught a break and need to do multi-location stakeouts. I'm afraid I won't be able to help escort Catherine."

"I understand that case has to take priority." The news was disconcerting. This made Catherine all the more vulnerable once she left the office. Maybe they could get help from local law enforcement.

One thing he knew for sure, staying here alone was not a good idea either.

SEVENTEEN

Catherine lifted the satchel off the floor where she'd placed it in the break room. She pulled her phone out. All through eating her dinner, her thoughts had been about Victoria. By going to the safe house, it felt like she was giving up on her sister. Victoria was out there somewhere…alone.

She dialed Andrea's number. Andrea picked up after the second ring.

"Hello?" Classical music played in the background.

"It's me, Catherine."

"Oh, Catherine. Let me turn the music down so I can hear you better." The music grew softer. "How's it going? Were you able to make contact with your sister?"

"No, long story, I was wondering if she's been back in touch with you."

"Not since I relayed the message about the coffee shop," said Andrea.

"Do you have the last phone number she called you from?" It was a long shot since Victoria was using burner phones but maybe she hadn't discarded the last one.

"I can look that up. Give me a second." After a moment, Andrea recited the number.

Catherine had a pen and paper ready to write it down. "Thank you."

"I hope you are able to help her."

"Me too," said Catherine. "Thanks, Andrea." She pressed the disconnect button and stared at the number she'd written down. If she still had the same phone, Victoria would recognize Catherine's phone number. Would she even pick up?

After a deep breath, she pressed in the numbers, feeling tightening at the back of her neck while the phone rang.

"Catherine?" Victoria sounded out of breath.

There was no time for small talk. "Victoria, you need to turn yourself in. This has gone on long enough."

"I don't know who to trust." Her sister's voice was filled with anguish.

"Please at least meet with me. I want to hear your side of the story."

"It didn't work out last time we tried. I could have been killed. I don't know what to do." Desperation colored Victoria's words.

"They took the man into custody who came after you. The man who saw you at the coffee shop."

"That man was hired by the man who is after me. Tristen will just send someone else," said Victoria. "He wants me dead because I can identify him."

Fear shot through Catherine at the realization that they were no safer than before. "What are you talking about? Who is Tristen?"

Victoria's voice faltered. "It's so complicated. Tristen knows powerful people in law enforcement."

Her sister sounded upset, and it seemed she was not going to get a clear answer from her. She had to do what she could to end being hunted by the men who were after Victoria. "Victoria, they're coming after me. They think I am you. This has to stop."

"I didn't realize. I didn't mean to put you in danger." Her voice got softer. "I'm innocent, Catherine."

"If you are innocent, you can turn yourself in."

There was a pause on the line as though Victoria was thinking about what Catherine said. "Where are you right now?"

Was Victoria considering meeting her? "I'm at the FBI field office in Bozeman. Please, Victoria, turn yourself in."

"Be careful around Agent McCloud."

She gripped the phone tighter as her stomach twisted. There it was again, the assault on Ryan's character. "Ryan is a good agent?"

Noise came through the line that sounded like a honking horn. "I have to go."

"Victoria, please."

The line went dead. She stared at the phone.

When Catherine looked up, Ryan stood in the doorway. There was a hardness in his expression. His jawline was stiff and his brows were drawn together. "You made contact with your sister?"

"Yes." She held the phone close to her chest. She understood why he was upset. She hadn't meant to go behind his back. She only wanted to know that her sister was safe.

"Dial the number again," he said. "Let me talk to her."

"Ryan, she doesn't trust you for some reason." Every time her sister said something about Ryan, it threw what she believed about him out of orbit. She had felt pulled between the two of them. More and more, spending time with Ryan made her realize that her sister might be wrong.

"Hand me the phone." His voice intensified.

She complied. He pressed buttons. A minute passed before he touched the disconnect button. Victoria had ditched the phone or wasn't answering.

"She says she's innocent," said Catherine.

"If that's the case, why doesn't she turn herself in?"

"You think my sister took those diamonds?"

"I withhold judgment until I have all the information. As long as your sister remains in hiding, I can't get that." A note of frustration colored his words. "She needs to come to me and tell me what she knows."

"She's afraid of you." Her voice softened. She saw what it did to him to have his character maligned. And she knew in that moment that he was an honest man trying to do the right thing. But could she open her heart to him or were the wounds just too deep for her? She felt a barrier there, a need to protect herself.

"I can't begin to know why that's the case." His voice held a note of anguish. He lifted his hand to give her back her phone. "The question is, do you trust me?" His gaze was unwavering.

She thought for a long moment before answering, knowing she had to be honest. "I know that you are a good agent. I believe that you want to keep me safe. Everything you've done indicates that. Please understand, trust in men is hard for me."

His jaw went slack and the light went out of his eyes. It was as if a curtain had fallen across his face. She read deep disappointment in his expression.

"We won't be making the drive alone to the safe house. Even though Agent Bronson got called away, I made a call. A city officer should be here soon. Are you ready?" His voice had taken on a neutral tone.

She stared at her phone. "By going to the safe house and then out of state, it feels like I'm giving up on my sister. I think she was almost ready to come out into the open. She asked where I was."

"You should have told me you were going to call her," said Ryan.

"I'm sorry." She rose to her feet. "I was worried about my sister. That's what was on my mind."

"I'm trying to run an investigation here."

"I know that. We just have different priorities." Her actions had hurt and upset Ryan. She was torn between wanting to help her sister and doing what Ryan thought was best. She felt like she was being backed into a corner. Right now, though, what choice did she have but to comply with his plan? "I'm ready to go if you are."

"Okay then," he said.

Ryan opened the door and made sure it locked behind him. They stepped outside and had only gotten a few feet from the building when gunshots broke the silence.

Plunging to the ground, Ryan covered Catherine's body with his own. He lifted his head, trying to discern where the shots had come from.

He rolled off her. "Quick, get behind that car." He pointed to the car closest to the building.

She crawled toward the front bumper of a compact car. Another shot reverberated in the air as he moved to follow her.

Adrenaline surged through his body when he peered above the hood of the car. He guessed at where the shot had come from. The shooter was nowhere in sight. "You have your phone. Call the police." He wondered too why the police escort hadn't shown up yet.

She pulled her phone out and pressed three numbers, her voice trembling as she spoke. "Please, we're outside the FBI field office building and we're being shot at."

The arrival of the local cops would scare the shooter away, but in the meantime, they had to stay alive.

He studied the other cars in the parking lot looking for any sign of movement. Then his gaze fell on the surrounding buildings. Traffic was light and there were no pedestrians close by.

The shot had sounded like it had come from a pistol, which meant the man must be close. It had to be Stephone Zander. Even if the man who had hired George sent someone else or came himself, he could not have set something up that fast.

They couldn't stay by this car. The man might reposition to get another shot at them.

"Let's make a run for it to my car." He patted her shoulder. "Can you do that?"

She nodded.

He watched the parking lot still thinking the shooter would show himself. There was one car between them and his SUV. "We go together. You stay on the left side of me." That way she would be shielded from the shooter. He pulled his gun from the holster.

"Okay," she said.

They sprinted to the first car without a shot being fired. With the gun in his hand, he lifted his head above the hood of the car. The stretch to get to his car would put them out in the open a few seconds longer.

Staying low and moving fast, they raced to his car. Catherine remained close to him. He pulled his keys out and clicked the unlock button. "Don't go around to the passenger side. Crawl through on the driver's side." The passenger side faced where the shooter probably was.

As he opened the door for her, he heard sirens in the distance. He got in. Just as he turned the key in the ignition, another shot was fired, piercing but not shattering a back window.

He saw Zander now. His head bobbed up from behind the trunk of the car as he took another shot.

Ryan turned the key in the ignition and pressed the gas. The car rolled forward but then rocked in an odd way as if the tires were square. One or more of the tires must have been shot out. He clenched his teeth. They weren't going anywhere. They were trapped with the shooter close by.

Time to play offense.

"Get down. I'm going after him." Ryan pulled his gun from the holster and pushed open the door.

Catherine unbuckled her seatbelt and slipped down to the floor of the car.

The man had moved in closer and taken up a position behind another car. Using his car as a shield, Ryan worked his way to the back bumper.

Zander was not raising his head at all.

The sirens grew louder.

With a backward glance to where the police were coming from, Zander burst out from behind a car and ran to the end of the parking lot.

One police car was only blocks away. That must be the escort who was already headed in this direction before the 911 call was made.

Ryan sprinted after Zander as he headed up an alley.

"FBI, stop!"

Zander ran faster and turned a corner. Ryan's feet pounded on the hard-packed dirt of the alley and then he stepped out onto the street where Zander had gone. He turned the corner just in time to see the man getting into the passenger side of a blue van. He must have a driver, someone else helping him. Ryan fired a single shot before the van had time to pull away from the curb.

He sprinted a short way, realizing the van was going too fast to fire at again with any degree of accuracy. He let his gun fall by his side. At least he knew what kind of vehicle Zander had acquired, and he'd gotten a partial read on the license plate. When he returned to the parking lot, the police had arrived, two patrol cars and three officers.

Catherine had gotten out of the car and was talking to an officer. Her head was bent, and she crossed her arms over her stomach. She looked in his direction as he made his way through the parking lot.

Ryan ran over to one of the officers who was watching the parking lot. "I'm Agent McCloud with the FBI. The woman over there and I were the ones who were shot at."

"I'm the officer who was supposed to escort you. Sorry for the delay. I got a call I had to take."

"The man who shot at us was in a blue van. He has an accomplice driving it. First numbers of the license plate 6F. He was headed south on Tracy Street."

"I'll call it in," said the officer. "Maybe we can catch him." The officer sprinted back toward his patrol car and pulled out his radio.

Ryan jogged over to stand by Catherine.

"I told the officer what happened." Her hand fluttered to her chest as she shook her head.

She was clearly torn up by the attack. He rested a hand on the middle of her back hoping to reassure her.

The police officer turned toward Ryan. "I'll need a statement from you as well."

Ryan recited what had happened and offered a description of Zander and the van he'd been driving.

The officer wrote down the details and excused himself.

Catherine stepped toward Ryan. "What do we do now?" There was a tremor in her voice as her eyes searched his.

He wanted to take her in his arms, to comfort her and quell her fear. Instead, he rubbed her arm.

"We can't go anywhere without a car. I'll call Agent Bronson and see if she can help us get another one. In the meantime, we go back into the field office and wait."

He feared that Zander might return. He knew Ryan's vehicle was disabled and that they would be stranded. "I'm going to see if some of the officers can stay in the parking lot until another agent can get here or at least get us another car. If we can get a car, one of the officers can escort us."

The field office was no longer a secure place for them to stay for any length of time, but right now, they had no choice.

EIGHTEEN

Still unable to calm down over the attack, Catherine waited by the field office door while Ryan spoke to one of the police officers. He patted the officer on the shoulder and turned to walk toward where she was. After Ryan swiped a card key he must have gotten from another agent, they stepped into the office together.

Ryan pulled his phone out. "I have to call the other agents."

Catherine sat in the chair in the front office. Ryan paced up and down the hallway while he made several calls. She caught only bits and pieces of the conversation.

She tried to take in a deep breath to release some of the tension from her body. She rose from the chair and gave a quick glance out of the office's window. She was glad to see that two of the police officers had stayed behind in the parking lot.

Ryan stepped into the front office. "Don't stand in front of that window."

She stepped away. "Sorry, I forgot."

"Good news. Agent Bronson can get relieved of her surveillance job and drive us to the safe house. It is just going to take a while."

"Good thing those police officers are parked outside," she said.

"Yes, for sure. Agent Bronson will let the officer know he no longer needs to escort us." They didn't seem to have much to say to each other. He angled his body slightly to stare up the hallway. "Why don't I pour you a cup of coffee?"

"That would be nice, thank you."

"You like cream and sugar?"

"Sure," she said. The gesture indicated that Ryan wanted to try to get along.

She sat in the quiet room twisting the strap of her satchel. Ryan returned holding two paper cups with steam rising out of them. He handed her one of the cups and took a seat opposite her.

What could they even talk about while they waited? Any conversation about the investigation was a land mine for conflict.

She took a sip of the warm liquid, appreciating the sweetness of the sugar and the sharp bite of the coffee. "Thank you for the coffee." She wiggled in her seat and took another swallow of coffee.

"You're welcome." He rose from his seat and paced toward the front desk and then back toward her. "You doing a little better? I know that was scary."

She touched her palm to her heart remembering the sound of the gunshots. "We came close to being hit with a bullet."

"I wish I could have caught him. At least I know he's driving a blue van."

Zander probably knew they were at the field office still without transportation. Would he be watching from a distance? Hopefully, the police presence would keep him away.

Ryan pulled his phone out of his pocket. "I'm going to call a towing place and make arrangements for the tires to be fixed on my car. Maybe Agent Bronson can see that it gets to the safe house. I don't want to be without a car."

She listened while he made the call. Another twenty minutes passed.

She'd just finished her cold coffee when Agent Bronson stepped into the front office.

"Heard you had some excitement here," said Agent Bronson.

Catherine nodded.

"We need to get out of here quickly," said Ryan.

Agent Bronson dangled her keys. "Let's go then."

Catherine took in a deep breath as they stepped outside once again, her gaze darting everywhere. The tow truck had already arrived for Ryan's car and the two officers had left. Agent Bronson got behind the wheel of her car. Catherine sat in the back while Ryan took his place in the passenger seat.

In the evening twilight, Catherine craned her neck to peer out the back window. She didn't see a blue van anywhere or anyone who looked like Stephone Zander. As they drove through town, though, she noticed a white sports car that always seemed to be behind them.

"It's a bit of a drive to get to the safe house. I'm going to have to stop and get some gas."

"I'll stay in the car with Catherine," said Ryan. His hand brushed over where his gun was underneath his jacket.

Agent Bronson got out of the car to fill up the tank. There were no other cars at the gas station. A lone clerk stood behind the counter in the well-lit convenience store.

Her stomach tensed as she realized how vulnerable they were when they weren't moving. She saw then that the white sports car was parked across the street. The driver was not visible in the evening twilight.

"I keep seeing that car," she said.

Ryan looked in the direction she was pointing. "Interesting. I don't think Zander could acquire another vehicle that quickly, but maybe his accomplice had one ready to go."

Agent Bronson finished fueling up and got behind the wheel. She pulled out onto the city street.

As she moved through city traffic, her eyes went to the rearview mirror. Catherine peered through the back window. No white sports car.

Once they got away from the city lights, it was too dark to see the make and model of the cars behind them.

When they arrived at the safe house, two cars drove past them, presumably headed to houses up the road.

"Can you stay and provide some extra protection?" Ryan asked. "I don't like being here without a car."

"I'll stay as long as I can. Unless I am called out to deal with that drug deal surveillance. So far, we haven't been able to spot the man we're trying to take in. I wonder if he got wind of our operation."

Catherine felt a weariness as they entered the house. She said good night and chose the room on the ground floor.

After a quick shower, she slipped under the covers and closed her eyes, wondering if they would be safe through the night.

When Ryan woke up the next morning, he found Agent Bronson in the kitchen already awake. She sat at the table with her phone and a mug in front of her.

"I put a pot of coffee on for you two," she said.

He searched several cupboards before finding the cups and pouring himself some coffee.

Agent Bronson pointed at her phone. "I have good news about a more permanent location for Catherine."

He sat down kitty-corner from her and reached for the sugar bowl that was on the table. "You got something set up?"

"Agent Martin did. A place opened up in California. She can leave on a plane this afternoon. An agent will meet her there to escort her on the flight and another agent will meet her when she lands for transport."

"That was fast. I want to go with her to the airport," said Ryan. The thought of saying goodbye to Catherine made him sad. Though he knew this was the safest thing for her, the idea of being away from her made his heart ache. Would he ever see her again?

Catherine stood in the doorway. "What are you talking about? Who's going to the airport?"

"We've got a safe place set up for you out of state," said Agent Bronson.

Catherine's jaw dropped. "I guess that's how it has to be." She ran her hands through her hair as her voice wavered. "I wish I could take the dogs with me or at least see them one more time."

"I don't think that's possible. We can't have you out in the open for long," said Ryan. "Hopefully, we can take the other suspect into custody and get some answers that will allow you to return here."

She slumped down in a chair.

"I'll wait around until your car arrives," said Agent Bronson. "The surveillance was a bust, so all the agents involved need to regroup in a bit."

Ryan rose from the chair, retrieved a cup and poured some coffee for Catherine, which he sat in front of her. The look on her face made his stomach tighten. That the situation had finally come to this was probably devastating to her.

She whispered a quiet thank-you and reached for the mug while she stared at the table.

Ryan forced cheerfulness into his voice. "Why don't I see what we have here for breakfast?" He turned back toward the cupboards.

"There's some cereal and some shelf-stable milk," said Agent Bronson.

"I'm not hungry." Catherine rose from the kitchen chair and wandered into the living room.

He wished there was something he could say to her. He searched the cupboards and found some breakfast bars.

"I think I'm going to step outside for a minute," said Agent Bronson.

She must have sensed that Ryan and Catherine needed to be alone.

He grabbed two breakfast bars and went into the living room where Catherine sat. Her untouched coffee rested on the table by the couch.

He put the breakfast bar beside the coffee cup. "You have to eat something."

"Where am I going?" She stared at the window with its drawn curtains.

"California." He sat down beside her.

"So far away from all that I know."

He draped his hand over hers where it rested on the couch. Her skin was soft to the touch and she did not pull away. "You were never supposed to be the target for these men. This whole thing has been so unfair."

"And what about my sister?"

Her question was a reminder of how sideways his mission had gone and also the deep concern Catherine had for her twin.

"Maybe once we take Zander in and Victoria realizes

she's not being pursued, she'll be willing to come out in the open. If she's innocent like she said, the smart thing to do would be to contact the bureau. Even if she doesn't trust me, she could contact another agent."

Catherine lifted the granola bar from the table and removed the wrapper. "I guess it will be the end of us being together too. I won't see you again."

"Yes, I guess so." So much was going unsaid between them. He had come to admire her strength. But also, he felt an attraction to her, though he doubted the feeling was mutual. Bottom line, she still did not fully trust him. Without trust, love was impossible.

"You'll be going back to Seattle after all this is over?"

"Yes." Yet another reason there couldn't be anything between them. They lived in different worlds.

She ate her breakfast bar. He sat beside her eating his and not speaking. An hour went by as they took turns pacing the room and getting cups of coffee until his car showed up and Agent Bronson excused herself.

Ryan's phone rang. Agent Martin. "Yes."

"We got an ID on the man George called, a Tristen Davis, owns several jewelry stores in the northwest."

"Interesting," said Ryan.

"We put a man on him to tail him, and he boarded a flight this morning headed to Bozeman."

He tensed. "I have to take Catherine to the airport."

"We plan on meeting his plane as soon as it lands and taking him into custody," said Agent Martin. "It's a busy airport. The chances of an encounter are low."

"All the same, I'm glad we have an agent going with her. I'll breathe a sigh of relief when that plane is in the air." He would feel better about her being in a safe place but not about never seeing her again.

"Like I said, we should be able to take him in quickly. The drug surveillance is suspended for now and we have lots of resources to put on this."

"Thanks for letting me know." He disconnected from the call.

He found Catherine in the kitchen where she was washing her coffee cup. "It's time to go. You'll be getting there early with plenty of time to board and meet up with the agent who's flying with you."

After setting the cup in the dish rack, she turned to face him.

The look on her face made him want to take her into his arms to comfort her. Her eyes rimmed with tears. He stepped toward her, and she fell into his arms.

"I hate that it has come to this." She rested her face against his chest with her palm on his heart.

"I know." The heartache over her going away made his voice falter. "Catherine." He leaned back and put his fingers under her chin. His eyes searched hers as the pain of loss overwhelmed him. He wanted to be with her more than anything.

His lips found hers and he kissed her gently. She leaned into the kiss, wrapping her arms around his waist. As he held her, a sense of warmth and well-being surrounded him.

She pulled away still looking into his eyes. "I guess that was a goodbye kiss."

Though the kiss had made him light-headed, they both knew the situation was impossible. "We better get going."

He drove down the road out to the highway watching for signs that indicated where the airport was.

Catherine pointed at the rearview mirror. "That white car is behind us again. I saw it yesterday too."

"Are you sure?" There were plenty of white cars. "Can you tell the make and model?"

"No," she said. "Maybe I'm just paranoid because we've been followed so much."

The parking lot at the airport was quite full. Ryan found a parking space between two trucks that was some distance from the *departures* doors.

Ryan glanced in the rearview mirror just as he was about to open the door.

A blue van parked by their bumper, blocking the possibility of backing out.

In an instant, a man he didn't recognize was at his door pulling it open while another man, Stephone Zander, opened Catherine's door and dragged her out as she called out and struggled to get away.

Ryan reached for his gun as an object impacted with the back of his head. He felt dizzy and black dots filled his field of vision. His knees buckled and he crumpled to the ground.

He passed out but came to a second later. He heard shouting, the sounds of a struggle. A door slammed. And then the van pulled away. He noted the direction it had gone right before his world went black.

NINETEEN

Catherine tried to fight off the man who had grabbed her. He pulled one arm behind her back as she took her free hand and reached to scratch his cheek. He jerked his face away before she could make contact. Zander pushed her restrained arm up at the elbow, causing her intense pain, while he reached for her other arm and secured it by wrapping his arm around her waist.

She twisted her body in an effort to get away. Her flailing only made him tighten his grip on her as he dragged her toward the open door of the van. She didn't see any people close by. Shouting for help would be pointless.

She saw a flash of white out of the corner of her eye and heard the screech of tires. She angled her body just in time to see the open door of the white sports car and Victoria racing toward her.

"You get away from her," Victoria shouted.

The man who had knocked out Ryan came up from around the side of the van, hit Victoria on the back of the head and shoved her in the van.

"I'm seeing double," he said.

"Yeah, I don't know what's going on," said Zander. He pushed Catherine into the van beside her unconscious sister and then got into the back of the van himself. He slid the door shut while the other man got behind the wheel.

Catherine again reached out to hit Zander. He blocked the blow and then pulled wire from his back pocket and grabbed her hand. The two wrestled until he had wrapped the wire around her wrists, restraining her hands in front of her.

Teeth showing, he waggled a finger in front of her. "Don't try anything." He crawled into the passenger seat of the van.

Victoria lay on her side, her cheek pressed into the carpet of the van floor. Her eyes were closed. She looked lifeless. Catherine's breath caught in her throat as she whispered her sister's name.

Catherine reached out to touch Victoria's cheek and then feel for a pulse, angling her bound hands so she could touch her fingers to Victoria's neck. Skin pushed back against her fingers. Victoria was alive.

Gratitude flooded through her. Her sister had come to save her and taken an enormous risk to do so. Such action spoke volumes about how Victoria felt about her twin.

She nudged Victoria's shoulder but got no response.

The two men spoke in low tones. "I had no idea there were two of them," said Zander. "This complicates things."

"You're the boss," said the second man. "What do you want to do?"

"I need answers from the one who took the diamonds."

The second man who was behind the wheel spoke up. "We got to find a place to hide. Get this van out of sight. That Fed I knocked out might come to and call for help."

"Yeah and he might put an all-points bulletin on the van. We need to ditch this vehicle before we leave the air-port and get something else," said Zander. "Let's get this done quickly."

"How about over there?" The second man lifted his hand

from the wheel and pointed. "Doesn't look like there's anyone there."

Catherine lifted her head to try to see through the windshield but did not have a clear view of where the men were headed. There were no windows in the back of the van.

The noise the tires made changed as they left the pavement for dirt. After several minutes, the van pulled into a three-sided brick building that must be under construction. The fourth wall was several large tarps that flapped in the wind but concealed the van.

Zander got out of the passenger seat. The side door to the van slid open, and he grabbed Catherine by the collar. "What do you know about the diamonds?"

Her heart pounded as she saw the fury in the man's eyes. "I know they were stolen from the man who hired you. I didn't take them."

"Then your sister must have."

"No, she's innocent." Victoria had done some things that made her look guilty, but she would take her sister at her word.

Zander pulled Catherine from the van. "One of you is going to tell me where those diamonds are because one of you took them."

Victoria stirred.

"Get the other one tied up," said Zander.

Catherine was dragged to a stack of wood pallets. Wind caused the tarp on the building to flap open for a second. She could see heavy equipment outside, which mostly blocked the view of the airport some distance away.

Victoria now with her hands bound in front of her was propped so her back was to Catherine.

Zander addressed the second man. "You go get us another car. I'll take care of these two."

Fear stabbed through Catherine at the sight of the gun in Zander's hand.

"I'll see what I can do." The second man took off running toward where the tarps hung.

Zander walked to the open-sided part of the building and watched the other man disappear behind the heavy equipment.

Victoria's voice was groggy. "I'm so sorry you got dragged into this. I never intended that to happen."

"Why did you try to get in touch with me?"

"I was going to go deep into hiding. I needed your help and I wanted to let you know how sorry I was for the way I hurt you. You're the only one I trust."

"Ryan McCloud would have helped you."

"Back in Seattle I saw him being quite chummy with Tristen Davis, the man who hired George Willis to kill me. I thought Ryan was involved."

Now she knew who Tristen was. Not that it mattered now that it looked like she was going to die.

Zander had turned back around and was stalking toward them.

"I think he is an honest agent, Victoria."

"I just got so afraid. Tristen Davis, the man who is behind the smuggling, was my mentor when I first got into the jewelry business. I thought I could trust him."

Now she saw why her sister had done what she'd done and been so paranoid. "You didn't have to do this alone."

"Whatever happens to us," Victoria spoke in rapid-fire whisper, "I want you to know that I was sorry for the things I did to you, the betrayal. Having to be on the run made me realize what your life was like because of Dave. I treated money as more important than people. I see what matters most now is people, especially family. I was wrong."

Zander was only a few feet from them.

"I forgive you," said Catherine. Knowing that her sister's life had been in danger made her realize that she loved Victoria and wanted her in her life…if they got out of this alive.

"Quit jabbering." Zander kneeled down and put his gun to Victoria's head. "Now, are you going to tell me where those diamonds are?"

"I don't have them. But I think I know who stole them. Tristen Davis took them and started rumors that I was behind it. He's the one who has been smuggling gems in glass objects."

Zander gripped Victoria's elbow and lifted her off the pallets. "You lie. You know where those diamonds are, now tell me." He pointed the gun at Victoria's head.

Catherine's whole body jerked. "Don't shoot my sister."

"Then one of you better start talking."

Catherine saw rage in the man's eyes. One way or another, it was clear he intended to shoot them once the other man came back with a different car.

Hard, cold concrete pressed against Ryan's cheek as he regained consciousness. The back of his head felt like it was on fire and his mind fogged. Still a bit wobbly, he rose to his feet trying to piece together what had happened. When he saw the open passenger side door, he gritted his teeth and shook his head. Catherine had been kidnapped and taken in the blue van by Zander and his accomplice.

He reached for his phone as he stepped away from his SUV. A white sports car with the driver's side door open stood in the middle of a lane rather than in a parking space. He walked over to it wondering what it meant. Whoever left it here had been in a hurry. The car that had been following them. He closed the car door.

He dialed Agent Bronson directly. "I need some help out here at the airport. Catherine has been kidnapped, taken in the blue van." He could not subdue the anguish in his voice.

Agent Bronson responded. "We can alert police and highway patrol to be looking for them."

"I think we need to do a search of the airport too." He had only a faint memory of the direction the van had gone when he'd come to for a moment, but he was pretty sure they weren't headed for the airport exit. "I'm going to start that search right now."

"Shouldn't you wait for backup?"

"I don't think we have that kind of time." Catherine had been put in harm's way on his watch. He would do everything to keep her alive.

"We'll get there as fast as we can," said Agent Bronson. "We are on our way anyway to meet Tristen Davis's plane."

Ryan jumped in his car and backed out, turning in the direction he remembered the van going. He headed toward the airport searching for the blue van. He didn't think they would stay out in the open, and it was possible they had gotten turned around and left the airport.

Whatever it took, he had to find Catherine. Guilt plagued his conscience. He'd gotten her into this trouble in the first place, though she had never blamed him.

The airport consisted of a huge building where the commercial flights took off and another smaller control tower for private planes, part of which looked like it was under construction. There were various pieces of heavy equipment parked around unfinished buildings a little distance from the control tower.

As he rolled through the parking lot, he didn't see the blue van anywhere. It would sit higher than other cars and should be easy enough to spot.

Out of the corner of his eye, he saw the man who had knocked him unconscious skulking through the parking lot checking to see if doors were locked on parked cars. Before he was spotted, Ryan backed into a parking space where he had a view of the man as he wove between the cars. He was clearly intending to steal a car.

The man finally found success with a battered orange truck that had a topper.

Slouched down in the driver's seat, Ryan watched the man back out and head past the commercial part of the airport toward the area of the private airport that was under construction. The orange truck stood out and it was easy enough to follow it with his eyes until it disappeared by the part of the private airport that looked to be under construction.

Ryan turned the key in the ignition and followed the same path the man had gone on. Once on the far side of the private airport, he saw several half-finished gray brick buildings. It looked like one was intended to be hangars for several planes.

Ryan parked some distance away, pulled his gun and got out of his vehicle. He moved toward where the incomplete hangars were. Two of the hangars still didn't have plane-sized doors on them and were empty with only a concrete floor.

He phoned Agent Bronson and told her where he was and about the orange truck. "I think they're hiding out here somewhere. I'm going in to look."

"We're within minutes of being at the airport. Wait for backup."

He knew waiting might cost Catherine her life. "Get here as fast as you can."

"Three cars are on their way. We just got word that

Tristen Davis's plane has landed. Hopefully, the agent on scene will take him into custody."

Ryan pressed the disconnect button and hurried around the hangar. There was another brick building with tarps hanging over one side of it. A good place to hide. The heavy equipment blocked much of the view of the building. He hurried around a bulldozer and circled the building, finding the orange truck parked on the side of the building out of view.

Ryan moved in close to the open side of the building where he heard muffled voices.

"We should just kill them now," said a man's voice.

Another male voice replied, "One of them knows where the diamonds are."

The threat of the words chilled him as his back pressed against the brick wall. He angled his body and peered through a hole in the tarp. He had a limited view. The man who had knocked him out was pacing in front of two women with a gun in his hand.

Ryan twisted his head to try to see more. Stephone Zander must be around there somewhere. The second man moved away from the two women. Ryan's heart skipped a beat. Catherine and Victoria sitting back-to-back. It looked like they were restrained. Catherine hung her head and her hair fell over her face. His breath stuck in his throat when he saw her.

The second man lifted Catherine up and put the gun to her head. He glared at Victoria. "Tell me where the diamonds are or your sister gets it."

TWENTY

Catherine's heart raged inside of her chest as the cold metal pushed against her temple. She prayed.

Lord, keep us safe.

"No, please." Victoria's voice filled with agony. "I'm telling you. A man named Tristen Davis took the diamonds and made it look like I had done it. He sent a man to kill me. You have to believe me. Don't hurt my sister."

Catherine struggled to take in a breath.

Stephone Zander stood close to Victoria. He had holstered his gun. He shook Victoria's shoulder. "Sure, we believe you." His voice dripped with sarcasm. "Where are the diamonds?"

A gunshot reverberated through the building. Catherine flinched. Her ear hurt from the intensity of the blast. The gun had been fired from outside. When the wind blew one of the tarps up, she caught a flash of movement by the open wall of the building.

The second man backed away from her, gripping his hand where he'd been shot. The gun fell on the concrete floor. He doubled over in pain.

Zander reached for his gun just as Ryan stepped out in the open. "FBI. Put your hands in the air."

Zander complied with Ryan's command.

Gratitude and relief coursed through Catherine when she saw Ryan.

Ryan's focus was on Zander. "Pull your gun and drop it on the ground, kick it toward me...nice and slow."

The man reached toward his holster and Ryan moved in closer, keeping his arms straight and his gun aimed.

The second man still held his wounded hand close to his body and grimaced. Reaching with his uninjured hand, the second man dove for his gun where it had fallen.

"No, you don't." Catherine hit him on his back with her bound hands then kicked the gun toward Ryan.

Ryan shifted focus to the second man. "Hands in the air."

The second man gingerly lifted his injured hand, which was still bleeding but not profusely. The bullet must have grazed him. "This was supposed to be a quick job." He spoke through gritted teeth.

Victoria, whose back was to the action, craned her neck.

Through the tarps, Catherine could see a marked FBI vehicle zooming toward them. Agent Bronson got out with her gun drawn. A second vehicle was right behind the first. Two more agents got out and approached the building.

Keeping his eye on Zander and the second man, Ryan spoke to the agents. "These are the two men who have been after Catherine."

Agent Bronson stepped through the tarps. "Looks like you have things well in hand." Agent Bronson addressed the other agents. "Take these men into custody."

The other two agents handcuffed Zander and the second man and escorted them toward one of the vehicles.

Ryan holstered his weapon and stepped toward Catherine, reaching to untwist the wire that bound her hands in front of her. Once her hands were free, Catherine wrapped her arms around Ryan as joy surged through her.

"Thank you for coming. I was afraid it was the end." She nestled against his chest breathing in the woodsy scent of his skin.

"No way was I going to let that happen." He squeezed her tight for a moment and brushed his hand over her hair.

Agent Bronson touched Ryan's shoulder. "We've only got two agents looking for Tristen Davis in the airport. I need to get over there and assist."

Ryan nodded. "I'll escort these two to the office. I don't think there's a need to put Catherine on that plane. I don't want to risk an encounter with Tristen while he's in the airport."

Agent Bronson hurried back to her car.

Victoria had scooted herself sideways on the pallet so she could see better. Catherine kneeled on the floor to remove the wire restraints from her sister's wrists. Victoria narrowed her eyes at Ryan.

"You have some explaining to do," said Ryan.

Victoria drew her hands in front of her and massaged her wrists. "I'm not sure I want to talk to you."

Catherine squeezed her sister's shoulder. "Victoria, whatever you think, I am telling you that Ryan can be trusted. He is one of the good guys." She looked right at him. "I trust him." More than believing in him as an agent, she trusted him with her heart.

A gentle smile graced Ryan's features. The look on his face warmed her to the marrow.

Victoria studied him for a long moment. "After so many betrayals, I just didn't know if you were playing me or one of the good guys."

"Victoria, the FBI wants to arrest the men who targeted you. I can guess at how this all went down," said Ryan. "Tristen Davis took the mafia's smuggled diamonds."

"Yes and started a rumor that it was me. Tristen knew I had figured out what he was up to and could identify him, so he sent George Willis to kill me." Victoria sounded as though she were about to cry. "George was a sometime courier for the jewelry stores. He always struck me as being kind of a shady guy."

Catherine looked toward Ryan. "Tristen was Victoria's mentor when she first got into the gem business."

"Tristen had some law enforcement in his back pocket," said Victoria. "I guess I projected that onto you."

She understood now why Victoria's trust in law enforcement had been so broken.

Ryan nodded. "I'll need to officially interview you and take your statement," he said.

Catherine sat down beside her sister and wrapped her arm around her. "Was Tristen smuggling diamonds by fashioning them into glass-looking objects?"

"Yes, I took the figurines as evidence," said Victoria. Her sister rested her head on Catherine's shoulder. "Quite a day."

Hopefully, it would all be over soon. Ryan's phone rang. He stepped away to take the call.

He turned sideways. His expression, mouth drawn into a tight line, looked grim.

Catherine wondered what had happened.

Ryan pushed a button on the phone and walked back toward the two women. "They still haven't located Tristen Davis."

"He couldn't have left the airport that quickly," said Victoria.

Ryan probably wished he could be part of the action instead of watching over the two women.

Catherine felt a tightening through her chest. "That means he's still out there."

"They're going to continue the search. It's a big, busy airport."

"They have to find him," Victoria said. "He will stop at nothing to kill me."

Ryan holstered his gun. "Let's get the two of you out of here."

"I need to get my car," said Victoria. "I'll follow you in."

Ryan hesitated. Given her history, could he trust her to do what she said?

Catherine gave him a nod of assurance.

"Okay, let's load up," he said.

They got into his car with Catherine in the passenger seat and Victoria sitting in the back. He drove through the construction zone past the private airport where a plane had just landed. They found Victoria's car where it had been left.

"Good, it hasn't been towed yet," said Catherine.

Victoria got out of the back seat and headed toward her car. She pulled the keys from a pocket.

A man came from between cars, grabbed her and put a knife to her throat. He yanked the keys out of her hand. Ryan recognized Tristen Davis. He must have recognized Victoria's car. Of course, he had a knife. There was no way he could have brought a gun on the plane. A knife might be easier to conceal.

Catherine gasped.

Ryan pulled his gun and hurried to get out of the car. He had time to open the door and draw his weapon just as the man pushed Victoria into the driver's seat. The man hurried around to the passenger seat. Ryan advanced on him, but Tristen ducked down using the car as a shield and got in.

As the white car sped away, Ryan sprinted back to his vehicle and jumped behind the wheel. The white car wove through the rows of vehicles. He lost sight of it behind some big trucks.

Was there a way to cut him off before he got to the exit?

Ryan tossed his phone to Catherine. "Call Agent Bronson. Tell her what's happening."

He listened to Catherine's frantic voice as he drove past each line of cars scanning the area for the white car. Was he hiding? Had he pulled in and parked somewhere in order to kill Victoria?

"There." Catherine pointed two rows over. "I saw him roll by."

Ryan spotted him too. The parking lot was like a labyrinth, but it was clear the white car was headed toward the exit. Ryan sped up.

He could see the white car as it closed in on the kiosk where an attendant waited to take payment for parking. The white car drove through the barrier. Ryan followed.

The car was nearly to the airport exit. Traffic was moderate as they went through the first roundabout. The car turned onto the frontage road.

Ryan drew close to the back bumper as the car slowed when it came up to another car moving below the speed limit. The white car took a sudden turn at an underpass. Tires squealing Ryan cranked the wheel, barely letting off the accelerator.

The turn took them into a residential neighborhood. The white car never slowed despite the reduced speed limit. Ryan stayed close, fearing a collision with another car or pedestrian. He was grateful when he saw an open field up ahead.

He pressed the gas to the floor and got alongside the white car. Victoria, her pale face like granite, gripped the wheel.

Catherine placed her hand on the dashboard bracing for impact.

He swerved, hitting the other car. It rolled off the road, into the field and impacted with the fence. Tristen got out and ran around to the driver's side of the car, pulling Victoria out and holding the knife to her throat.

Ryan's heart raged in his chest as he pulled his gun and advanced on Tristen.

Victoria's eyes were wild and terrified. Her body blocked the possibility of him being able to shoot Tristen.

Catherine had come up beside him. In his peripheral vision, he saw her shake her head ever so slightly while she looked at Victoria. Some sort of signal between sisters?

Victoria stretched her hand to scratch Tristen's face. He drew his free hand up to the wound allowing her time to angle her body away from him. Tristen lurched to grab her.

Catherine picked up a rock and threw it at Tristen's head, hitting her target.

The move was enough to stun him so Victoria could step out of his reach.

Ryan arced around so he had a clear shot at Tristen. "Drop the knife, right now."

Victoria stumbled forward and fell into her sister's arms. It was over. All the men who had come after Catherine were in custody. Ryan knew he'd be on a flight back to Seattle within a day.

Catherine sat in the reception area of the field office while Ryan took a full statement from Victoria in one of the interview rooms. The plan was for her and her sister to drive out to the farm after they were done here. Victoria was considering staying in Montana.

If the charges against her ex-husband stuck and he went to prison, Catherine could hope to move back to the farm once Ralph's lease was up.

It looked as though she might get back her old life and yet she felt a deep chasm. Ryan would be returning to Seattle.

Ryan and Victoria walked along the hallway toward her as she got to her feet. His magnetic gaze made her take a step toward him.

"All done?"

He nodded. "Yes, the investigation is closed."

What did she hear in his voice? Sadness?

Victoria cleared her throat. "You know, I think I'll take a step outside for some air and to enjoy my new freedom." She winked at Catherine as she stepped past her.

Catherine let out a half laugh. Her sister saw the attraction between them. Catherine waited until the door closed behind Victoria.

Locking him in her gaze, she took a step toward him trying to read his expression. "Guess she wanted to give us a chance to say goodbye alone."

Double lines appeared between his eyebrows as he patted her arm. "I've already got my plane reservation for early tomorrow."

"I know your life and your work are in Seattle, but I'm going to miss you." She studied the deep blue of his eyes.

His voice grew thick with emotion. "I'll miss you too."

She fell into his arms relishing the warmth and the safety of being close to him, knowing it couldn't last.

He kissed her forehead and then her lips, tenderly brushing over her mouth. The soapy cleanness of his skin surrounded her as she longed for the moment to last forever.

"You're one of a kind, Catherine. I'm not going to forget you."

She rested her hand on his heart, feeling it beating. "Take care."

He brushed his knuckles over her jaw, leaned in and kissed her. The touch of his lips on hers was bittersweet.

Lifting her hand from his chest, she pulled away and turned toward the door. She gave herself one more backward glance at the man she'd come to care for so deeply. The man who had restored her trust.

"I won't forget you either." She reached for the door and stepped outside where Victoria was waiting, feeling like so much had gone unsaid between her and Ryan.

TWENTY-ONE

"How's my girl doing?" Catherine kneeled down to pet a very pregnant Betty. From the porch of the farmhouse where she stood, she had a view of part of the farm. Victoria, with Liz trailing behind her, made her way to the barn. Once Ralph and Celeste's lease was up on the farm, she and Victoria had made the decision to resume the work their father did breeding and training border collies.

Ralph continued to lease some of the fields to plant crops.

She peered out at the road expecting to see a car any minute. Her ex-husband had stood trial and been convicted of kidnapping and attempted murder thanks to Ryan's testimony. They had had very little chance to talk during the trial, and he had promised to come by the farm to say good-bye. Ryan had texted her that he was running late due to some business he needed to take care of.

Betty followed her down the steps hindered by her bulging belly. A car appeared in the distance. She shaded her eyes from the sun as her heart fluttered.

Seeing Ryan caused a mix of emotions. He had spent these months back in Seattle where his life and his work were, and he would return to the city after their visit.

Being with him at the trial had reminded her how much she had come to care about him, maybe even love him.

Time and distance had not caused the intensity of the feelings to fade.

The car slowed as it got closer to the house and then stopped not too far from where she stood.

Ryan smiled and waved before opening the door and stepping out.

"Good to see you." She held her hands open to him and they embraced awkwardly. Not one of the warm hugs they had previously shared. Perhaps he didn't want to send her any mixed signals.

Betty wagged her tail and Ryan gave her an enthusiastic pet on the head. "She looks ready to burst." He glanced around. "You and Victoria are running the farm now?"

"Just the dog part of it. Ralph is still taking care of planting and harvesting the crops."

She showed him around, stopping to talk to Victoria and then inviting him in for some iced tea and cake. Ryan seemed distant, as though his thoughts were elsewhere.

She set the tea and cake in front of him and then poured a glass for herself and sat across from him. Betty rested on the floor covering Catherine's feet with her belly.

Ryan had been quiet while they walked around the farm. Maybe for him the attraction between them had died.

He took a bite of the cake. "I'm glad you're settled into your life here and you and Victoria can work together."

"Yes, it's been good for both of us. I have had to do some work and heavy praying to learn to forgive her for past hurts. I want us to be as close as we were before our parents divorced."

Ryan nodded while he stared at the table.

Was there something he wanted to say but was holding back?

She filled the silence with what she thought was a benign question. "How's life in the big city?"

He reached over and covered her hand with his. The warmth of his touch seeped through her skin. His expression seemed to change. The hard mask fell away and light came into his blue eyes. "It's empty without you."

The intensity of his words took her aback. Her heart skipped a beat. "What are you saying?"

"I'm sorry if I seemed cold. My mind has been going in a thousand directions." He squeezed her hand. "The reason I was delayed was because I visited the Bozeman field office."

She shook her head. "I don't understand."

"I wanted to find out if there was a slot opening up for an agent, to see if I could transfer here."

She couldn't fully process what he was saying. "You want to move to Montana?"

"I want to be close to you. Seeing you at the trial made me realize I care about you, Catherine. I'd like to get to know you better. I missed you all these months. Thought of you often."

She gushed. "I missed you as well." The idea was a revelation to her. Despite the safety and happiness she now enjoyed, there had been a hole in her life without him. "It has been wonderful being back at the farm with my sister, but I felt an emptiness too."

His eyes searched hers. "There will be an opening in a few months. One of the older agents is retiring. I can get a job here if that's what you want."

Feeling a rush of joy, she pushed her chair back and stood up. Betty moved away but remained laying down. Of course, that was what she wanted. She nodded. "Yes, I would like that."

He stepped toward her, taking both her hands in his. "Catherine, I love you. There, I said it."

She fell into his arms, relishing the embrace. "I love you too." She pulled back and gazed into his eyes. "There, *I* said it."

He leaned in and kissed her, brushing his lips over hers and deepening the kiss. Nourished by his touch, she melted in his arms.

He lifted his head and gazed at her. "We weren't together long before. We'll take it slow and get to know each other in a deeper way, but I am hoping to make you my wife."

"Oh, Ryan. We can build a life together here." Her spirits soared. This is what she had wanted all along. To be in the place she loved with the man she loved.

"You're saying yes, you will marry me?"

"Yes, I will marry you. There, I said it."

He took her in his arms and kissed her again.

Betty barked her approval.

* * * * *

If you enjoyed this story,
Check out other titles by Sharon Dunn
Available now on LoveInspired.com!

Dear Reader,

I hope you enjoyed the danger and adventure that Ryan and Catherine faced as they were falling in love. As I wrote this book, I saw the theme of trust emerging. Catherine's trust in men has been broken by an abusive marriage. She must learn to see that Ryan is different. She has been thrown into a world of danger that was not because of anything she has done. She must trust that God is still in control, even though circumstances would say otherwise. In my own life, I have found that when trials, suffering and struggles come, there is an enormous opportunity to lean into God and trust him in a deeper way. This past year while I wrote this book, I have been undergoing treatment for cancer. So far, the outcome looks to be a good one. Did I completely trust God and not give in to confusion and anger? Not always. But I did try to make it a moment by moment practice to turn all my fears over to God and to thank Him for the opportunity to grow more dependent on Him, to believe in his faithfulness when circumstances seemingly contradicted that. As long as we are this side of heaven, all of us will face trials of one kind or another. I pray that through your difficulties, you would see the opportunity God has put before you. I love hearing from readers you can contact me through my website at www.sharondunnbooks.net.

Sincerely,
Sharon Dunn

and felt under her one of the cups and took a seat